A Thornton Brothers Time Travel Romance Novel
Book 4

Cynthia Luhrs

This book is a work of fiction. Names, characters, places, and incidents either are products of the author's imagination or are used fictitiously.

Last Knight, A Thornton Brothers Time Travel Romance Novel

Copyright © 2016 by Cynthia Luhrs

Acknowledgments

Thanks to my fabulous editor, Arran at Editing720 and Kendra at Typos Be Gone.

Chapter One

Present Day—Late October

There should have been a sign or some faint inkling that warned Ashley Bennett her well-ordered life was about to come crashing down like shards from a plate dropped on a tile floor. But nope. The powers that be were silent, content to let her go about her day, blissfully ignorant of the vortex of chaos lurking, waiting for the worst possible moment to destroy life as she'd known it these past twenty-three years.

Why was it dark? Was there a storm coming? With a frown, she glanced at her watch.

"No, no, no."

Ashley jumped, knocking the mountain of paper from her desk onto the floor of her office and sending the chair rolling out the doorway, where it hit the pristine white walls with a bang. Cashmere coat dangling off one arm, she gathered up the outrageously expensive buttery leather tote, shoving papers haphazardly inside while peering across the hallway to stare out the floor-to-ceiling windows. While she and Mitch each had an office, it was an interior office without windows. Only the big executives got views.

The darkness showcased fat white flakes striking the glass, suspended in time before each one died, turning into water and sliding down the window.

"I'll never get a cab in this weather."

Even worse. She was talking to herself. Out loud. Her coworkers would think she'd lost it...though by the looks of things, they'd done the smart thing and left hours ago.

This merger had taken over her life. Determined to make an impression and vault the corporate ladder, she'd put in sixteen-hour days, seven days a week, at the biggest hedge fund in the city, each and every day since she'd graduated. Top of her class, thank you very much. Though all those hours would be wasted if she didn't watch her back.

The elevator doors shut with a hiss, reflecting her face endlessly in the mirrored surfaces. Instead of music, industry news droned on, and she half listened as she furiously typed responses to the emails not so patiently waiting in her exploding inbox. Something about the earliest recorded snowfall on record caught her ear. She hated snow. For that matter, she hated wind and rain too. Give her an artificially climate-controlled environment any day. Her heels echoed across the marble lobby.

"Miss Bennett?"

The night security guard waved. "Your cab is waiting out front."

"Jonas, you're a lifesaver. I figured there'd be about as much chance of me getting a cab as Jersey has of winning tomorrow." She leaned on the high desk. "How'd you know?"

He pointed to the clock. "You've been working late ever since I started. Knew you wouldn't want to ruin those pretty shoes in this weather."

The designer heels she'd almost come to blows over during a super-secret sample show a few weeks ago seemed to glow in the muted light. Ashley admired the beautiful shoes. Just wearing them made her feel invincible.

"You're the best. I would have been late to dinner."

Jonas made a point of looking at the ornate clock again. "One day you need to slow down and smell the flowers. The work will still be there in the morning."

"Flowers make me sneeze." As she wrapped an oversized scarf around her hair, she arched a brow at the guy. He was still in school. Working as a security guard helped him pay for college. She rummaged around in her bag, came out with an envelope, slid it across the desk, and watched his face.

He peeked inside and blinked at her. "Are those Rangers tickets?"

"Two front-row seats behind the penalty box."

He caressed the tickets then snatched his hand back.

"I couldn't accept them."

The cab honked. Ashley turned and held up a finger. "The cab tonight, pizza delivered for dinner last week, and a warning when Randy Andy was headed my way. You've more than earned them."

Jonas held up the tickets, looking at them as if they were a supermodel rising out of the floor. "Tomorrow night, my one night off."

The cab honked again. "I can't use them, so enjoy. I have to run or I'll be late."

"And we know how you can't deal with being late." He pressed the button to unlock the doors. "Thanks, Miss Bennett. You're the best."

Ashley waved, Jonas already forgotten as the ping of the phone announced a message from her boss. She'd set up different sounds, assigning the higher-ups their own sounds so she'd never miss a communication. While she firmly believed in taking the extra thirty seconds to be nice to doormen, assistants, and delivery guys, knowing it would pay off later, she really didn't like people all that much. More that she tolerated them, counting the minutes until they'd leave her alone to accomplish her plans and goals. Talking to people always seemed like so much work. Trying to figure out what to talk about and to listen, when she wanted to get back to her own work. Anyway, she had enough work as it was without befriending anyone.

Ensconced in the warm interior smelling faintly of cloves and feet, she gave the cabbie the address, using the time to return calls, check her calendar, and update her task list for tomorrow.

With two minutes to spare, she was seated at the table. First, as usual. Might as well put the time to good use. Busy reading through the report she had to turn in next week, she heard someone speaking to her.

"You might want to move your papers. Red stains." The server held up a glass of wine.

"Thanks. I'm sure my friend will be here soon. Would you

bring a glass of Chardonnay for her?" Shoving the stack out of the way to make room, Ashley checked the time.

"I'm here. I'm not that late."

Ashley slammed a hand down to keep the papers from flying off the table as the whirlwind, also known as Marsha, sat down.

A pointed look at her watch made her friend wince.

"I swear, you're always late. I'm going to start telling you we're meeting half an hour earlier, then maybe you'll show up on time."

"Wouldn't do any good. I'd still be late. Better use of all that pent-up energy would be for you to accept some people aren't glued to the clock like you are." She leaned in close, and Ashley resisted the urge to scoot back. "I still can't believe you nabbed those shoes. They are fabulous."

Ashley flexed her foot. "I love them."

"And your dress. Is that a Diane von Fürstenberg?"

"Yep. Classic wrap dress."

Marsha wriggled out of her coat. "You look fantastic. Have you ever looked into your genealogy? I'd bet a hundred bucks you're descended from Peter Henlein."

"Who?"

"You, the woman who has the most unnatural fixation with clocks I've ever seen, doesn't know Peter Henlein?" Marsha took a big gulp of wine, almost knocking over Ashley's glass in the process.

She steadied the glass then safely stowed the files and report away. There'd be time to finish it tonight before she went to bed.

"Okay, tell me. Who is he? The guy who invented the

bangle watch?" She held out her wrist. "They are rather fabulous."

Hers was hot pink and had *Clean Slate* engraved on the inside. It reminded her of where she'd come from, and no matter what, she was never going back.

"Close, but no. He was from Germany. A locksmith who supposedly invented the first watch. Though it weighed so much it had to be worn on a belt. I'm surprised you don't have a shrine to the guy in your apartment."

"Hilarious. It's important to be on time." She tapped the watch. "I know, you don't believe in being confined by time; you'd rather wake when the sun comes up and go to bed when it goes down. But for those of us who have to be on time, it's like dragging one of those metal folding chairs across a concrete floor."

"Really? That bad?"

Ashley shuddered. "Worse."

"Can't make any promises, but I'll try to be on time for our next dinner."

Knowing when to pick her battles, Ashley motioned the server over.

"Ready to order?"

The server brought more wine and a basket of bread while Marsha regaled Ashley with tales of her latest dating trials and tribulations.

"You are so lucky you have Ben." Marsha waggled her brows. "Talk about something nice to wake up to."

Before Ashley could answer, a sound drifted across the noisy open space, making her cringe. No matter how hard she'd tried to forget, Ashley would recognize the soft drawl anywhere. She'd spent a significant amount of money to erase any trace of her upbringing over the past several years.

Trying to look casual, she scanned the room. Should have known. The two women looked like bright peacocks in a sea of black and muted colors. They sat together, wearing lots of jewelry over their bright red and blue sweater dresses. Both of them were made up, and had that innocent yet sexy look. Southern. Without a doubt. They were oblivious to everyone around them, leaning toward each other, hands moving as they talked animatedly, no doubt about their trip to The City.

Ashley strained to hear. The redhead was talking about how many cans of tomatoes and beans she'd put up this summer.

"Look at them. Tourists." Ashley wrinkled her nose. "Who still cans food? I thought that went out with the Dark Ages."

"No kidding. Give me a jar of spaghetti sauce anytime. Better yet, let the delivery guy bring me dinner already prepared."

"I know, right? Talk about a lot of work."

Marsha cocked her head, watching the two women. "The summer I turned thirteen, my parents sent me to Kansas to spend time with my grandmother. She made me help her pickle and can beets. To this day, I can't stand beets. But I didn't think you knew anything about canning. Come to think of it, you've never said where you grew up. Spill."

Prepared, Ashley didn't squirm. Instead she met Marsha's curious gaze and said, "Buckhead. Our cook brought jars of sauce she canned when she made pasta for dinner."

Her friend's eyes widened a fraction before the jaded look

was firmly back in place.

"Talk about a ritzy part of Atlanta. Wish I had a cook and a maid growing up. My brother and I were the help at our house. Silver spoon and all that, huh?"

"Something like that. Seems so long ago."

"That how you snagged your fabulous apartment?"

"My parents weren't thrilled with me moving to the city, so we compromised. They'd help with a place to live in a neighborhood they approved of, and I'd take care of the rest on my own."

Marsha looked at the women, who were now laughing loudly enough to cause several tables to turn and stare.

"Glad you're not some hick from some rinky-dink town with one stoplight."

Ashley made an exaggerated show of shuddering.

"Can you imagine? How awful. Though thank goodness some people like to live out in the middle of nowhere. After all, if they all lived in the city, it would be even more crowded than it already is."

"No kidding. I'd be bartering my future children so I could afford rent on the closet I call home." Marsha drained her wine. "Not that I'd ever have kids, but you know."

"I do." With a lingering look at the tourists, Ashley clenched her hands together under the table, willing the shaking to stop.

Chapter Two

England—October 1334

Christian Thornton, Lord Winterforth, had spent the entire journey thinking on his betrothed. 'Twas past time for him to do his duty. Marry. Have children to carry on the title and Thornton name. In the three weeks since he left his home at Winterforth and rode through the gates at Ravenskirk, not once had he wondered if he might come to love his bride to be. Duty first. Always. Let his brothers marry for love; recent events had shown him love was not to be.

After losing several prospective brides, he and his brothers—well, in truth, Charlotte and Melinda—had taken matters in hand, declaring he would marry at Ravenskirk. Charlotte had muttered about placing extra guards on duty or tying the girl to a chair until the deed was done. Christian had tried not to take offense. Henry's wife was due to give birth any day, and her temper made even the fiercest of his brother's guard flinch under her sharp tongue.

Though as he looked at his brother's home, he noticed differences between Ravenskirk and Winterforth. The new tapestries on the walls, cushions on the chairs, and the clean floors. He had never worried about the state of his hall. But now he was to be married, his wife would want changes. Women desired their homes to look and smell lovely. As he was thinking about the changes she might desire to undertake, and how much gold it would cost, a voice startled him.

"You look as if you're off to the gallows this fine morn instead of meeting your intended." Edward cuffed him on the shoulder. "She is a good lass from a wealthy family. Look happy, or she may think you do not wish to wed her."

"If she is so delightful, why does she not run away like the others?"

"Hush, whelp." Christian's eldest brother leaned in close, trying to whisper. "Her dam has been ill and not heard the rumors. With a bit of extra gold, her sire was willing to ignore the foolishness of womanly gossip."

Edward scratched his nose. "He is eager to wed into one of the richest families in the realm." Then he smirked. "Best lock up the larder. His lady will eat everything, and you'll have nothing left to survive the winter."

If a wedding was to be a happy celebration, why did Christian wish to run home and draw up the bridge? Forget about duty and responsibility and find a girl who wanted the man, not the name or the gold. But he was a Thornton, so he would do what needs be done.

"When the girl hears what is being said about me, she will cry off like the others." Christian kicked at the dirt as he watched Henry train in the lists.

John joined them, wiping his brow. "Her sire will see the deed done. Now go inside and make yourself ready. You are to be married, and I for one am looking forward to seeing the last of the Thorntons wed."

"'Tis long past time. Even I wed whilst you've been dithering about." Robert swaggered up to them, grinning. "If I could marry, certainly you can find one bride in the realm to have you. Though you are puny, and not as handsome as I."

Christian narrowed his eyes. "If this one flees..."

"She will not," James said as he poured a bucket of water over his chest, the steam rising from his skin. "For if she does, Melinda has sworn to hunt her down and drag the girl back by her hair."

"Not if Lucy gets there first." William rocked back on his heels. "Marry the girl, get her with child, and put these ridiculous rumors to rest. Nothing more than idle gossip."

"From a powerful widow who crushes men beneath her pretty toes for sport. What was I thinking to bed her?"

"I've seen her. You likely weren't thinking clearly." Robert leered at Christian.

Christian cared for his family. A great deal. But at this moment the meddling bunch made him want to renounce them all and join the monastery. Did they allow the monks to ignore their prayers and spend their days fighting, hunting, and riding? Most likely not. Stretching to his full height, he decided. Once married, he would get his new wife with child and the rumors would fade away. A Thornton always fulfilled his duty.

"Shouldn't I at least speak to the girl afore we wed this day?"

A chorus of "nays" met his ears.

"Is she a terrible shrew? Or so ugly you needs keep her hidden?"

"Dolt." Edward sent him sprawling in the dirt.

Rolling to his feet, Christian came up swinging. James called out encouragement as Christian caught Edward in the face. Yet his brother merely grunted and tossed him into the water trough. Spluttering, he glared but failed to look fearsome as he caught sight of the blood running from Edward's nose and laughed. For a moment, he wished he had been born an only child.

It was only later he realized his brothers had never answered him as to his bride's visage.

Christian looked to his brothers, standing tall at the front of the chapel, dressed resplendently. The women had servants scurrying to do their bidding all day, covering the chapel in so much greenery he was surprised the trees were not all bare. The overwhelming smell of juniper made him sneeze. They had insisted his bride would wish the chapel to be pleasing. Women. Let them have their womanly things.

He shifted from foot to foot, wondering what was taking so long. His intended's dam was arguing with her husband as Christian strained to listen. The man grew red in the face, the discord causing Christian to pray he would not be ill all over his new tunic and boots.

The door opened with a bang, interrupting his thoughts, as he watched Melinda stomping toward him, followed by her sisters. Jennifer, Elizabeth and Anna trailed behind them and his stomach revolted.

It seemed everyone was in attendance except his bride to be. The women looked like a flock of birds, dressed in their finery; too bad the scowls on their faces took away from their loveliness. He risked a gaze at his brothers, and what he saw had him touching the blade at his side. Before James reached Melinda, she poked the man in the chest. Seemed he would not be Christian's father-in-law after all.

"Your wretched daughter has run off with one of the stable boys."

The girl's mother sidled away, but was stopped by Lucy brandishing one of the wooden sticks she used to make scarves. As Christian looked more closely, he saw a piece of yarn hanging from her skirts, hidden away in one of the pockets she and her sisters insisted in putting in every garment. When he'd asked, they blushed and said they didn't think such a small thing would have a very large impact on history—at least, they hoped not. Charlotte had laughed, saying she hoped whoever invented pockets would still invent them, but Melinda chimed in and said, "Perhaps he got the idea from us, and isn't that something to make you think?"

Christian did not think overmuch on future doings. He preferred to believe the women came from a faraway land, but not from the future. Thinking of the future made his head ache. His attention was pulled back to Melinda as she took the runaway bride's mother by the arm.

"Don't even think about sneaking out of here, lady."

Then the bellowing began. Not by him. Deep down he'd expected the girl to bolt. Whilst his family roared and made threats, Christian strode out of the chapel, stopping in the kitchens to pilfer some of Henry's best wine, then made for the stables, where he saddled a horse and rode out of the gates.

After the third one had run, Christian quit counting how many brides he had lost. Was this the fifth? Mayhap he should visit the abbey on his ride. In all his score and four years, he'd never raised a hand to a woman. Today he thought on the widow responsible for his current state of affairs, and his fingers twitched next to his blade as he remembered the embarrassment of confessing his shame to Edward.

"All because of one night." Christian leaned closer to Edward. "At court last year, a wealthy widow took me to her bed." He snorted. "The lasses always flock to my bed, and I had heard she did not want to marry only to enjoy the bed sport, so I eagerly followed her to her chamber."

Edward tapped his foot, trying to hide his impatience.

"I was deep in my cups and I... Bloody hell. I fell asleep. The next morn, she told all I suffered grave injury as a boy and could not have babes." He threw up his hands and paced. "None will have me. Each lass finds a reason why she cannot marry me, or their sires agree to the betrothal and the girl runs away. They would rather be beaten than face a life without children. I will die alone."

"You are Lord Winterforth," Edward said. "Not as handsome as I, and your swordplay is lacking, but you are a Thornton, and any would give much to ally with us. Marry a girl and put a babe in her belly that will end the rumors."

"Nay, Edward. The last one ran away to France to marry a baker rather than face me at the altar. I am doomed to loneliness."

Edward rolled his eyes. "Then put a babe in one of the serving wenches' bellies, give her a few coins, and stop this nonsense being spouted amongst the eligible maidens of the realm." Edward threw up his hands. "Hell, marry a foreign lass."

Christian was horrified. "I will have an English bride, and I cannot put a babe in a woman's belly on purpose. Father taught us to cherish all women. Not to ill-use them. A babe would be my responsibility. What do I know of raising a babe? 'Tis women's work." His shoulders slumped. "I cannot."

"Ask Charlotte or Anna. All of the women in our family enjoy meddling. Surely they can find you a wife who will not bolt before you have bedded her."

"And you? Why, then, have you not married, if 'tis so simple any dolt can do it?"

"I have been visiting eligible maidens, and soon I will choose one to become the lady of Somerforth."

Christian raised a brow.

"Harrumph. None have suited me thus far. All of them are much too biddable."

"I would gladly have a meek and quiet wife. One who will leave me to hunt."

Edward cuffed Christian. "Dolt. Do not let Melinda hear you say such, or she will swear to find you a shrew to plague you the rest of your days."

"You want a future girl? Now who is daft? There are none to be had. 'Tis not possible."

Done with thinking about the past, he urged his horse to a gallop. Christian rode until the dark mood dissipated. In a clearing, he came upon an abandoned hut. 'Twas gloomy and dusty inside, and he had to shoo away the vermin who had made their homes in the hovel. He would spend the afternoon wallowing. Robert said it did wonders, though now he was married, he no longer wallowed. Elizabeth did not hold with feeling sorry for oneself.

Christian held the wine up. "At least you never desert me." The horse shook his head and went back to grazing at the grass growing through the window where the wall had fallen down.

All of the Thornton men were considered handsome. Some of the most handsome man in the realm. While he did not consider himself vain, Christian knew his visage was pleasing. Women remarked on the color of his hair, saying it was like the sun shining on gold. They praised his eyes, saying they were as blue as the sea, and his teeth straight and white as snow. But today he felt as deformed and hideous as a troll living under a bridge from the old tales.

Was his temperament foul? Did he bellow overmuch? He did not think it so, but mayhap he should ask Lucy. Or perhaps Charlotte. She was more tactful in her replies.

Christian leaned back against a heap of rags, coughing as dust filled the room. He would drink and forget. Perhaps tomorrow would be better. After all, it likely couldn't get any worse, could it?

Chapter Three

The cold marble seeped through her yoga pants, chilling her, as Ashley sat on the pristine white counter, feet in the sink, eating cereal for dinner. The fuzzy pink socks looked like an old, worn towel as she tapped her toes to the music playing.

The best thing about living alone? No one fussed about feet in the sink or cared that she sat on the counter eating dinner. No one complained if she napped on the weekend or slept half the day away—not like she did, but still, it was nice to have the option. Because when she did take the rare day off? It was pajamas all day, binge-watching her favorite shows, and naps galore. Ashley answered to no one, not even Ben.

The spoon slipped out of her hand, clattering as it hit the dishes in the sink before coming to rest in a teacup. Abruptly, she put the bowl down, jumped off the counter, and went to lean against the window in the living room, looking out into the darkness, her reflection staring back. Resting her cheek against the cold glass, she wondered, why did the past always pick the absolute worst time to sit down for a spell? The smell of pancakes and bacon filled the room, overlaid with a kind Southern voice. Turning the lights out as she moved through the apartment, hoping to banish the memories, she found herself in the bathroom, water running, with no recollection of brushing her teeth. She had to touch the toothbrush to check. Sighing, she climbed into bed, flannel sheets warm against her skin as she tossed and turned for what seemed like hours. But sleep was nowhere to be found, not so close to Halloween.

Out of practice, huffing from the exertion, Ashley coiled the jump rope and stowed it in a wicker basket next to the sofa. Outside, big, fat, fluffy flakes were falling, and she smiled, watching a child dressed in a bright red coat and matching boots dart across the street, his mother trailing after him. She loved this neighborhood, adored her rent-controlled prewar apartment, and as she stood there thinking about two very different childhoods, Ashley swore she could smell hot chocolate.

There was a knock, the door opened, and in came her boyfriend bearing the source of the smell.

"I knew you wouldn't have time to grab one on the way in today." He handed her the hot chocolate. "Made sure they added extra whip." He peered closely at her before taking her wrist, his lips moving as he counted.

"Whoa. Have you been moving furniture? You're sweating and your face is really red." Ben looked around as if he should notice something out of place.

"Nope. Jumping rope. When I was a kid, I carried my jump rope with the purple handles everywhere. Picked up a new rope yesterday and thought I'd see if I still had it." She touched her side, pinching the bit of extra padding. "You know how it is around the holidays, all the extra food and drink, trying to avoid gaining five pounds."

She took a sip, the chocolatey goodness filling her mouth, the warmth traveling through her chest, flooding her body with contentment.

"Have I told you how perfect you are? Though I should lay off this stuff until January."

"Not for at least a day. I know how much you love hot chocolate."

Ben kissed her on the cheek, a whiff of cinnamon filled her nose, and she spotted the ever-present pack of gum in his shirt pocket. "And for the record, you do not need to lose five pounds. You're fine the way you are." He looked her up and down. "Unless you're planning to wear your Rangers jersey into the office, you're going to be late."

His comment ripped her out of the cobwebs of memory. "I can't believe I lost track of time. I never do that. You're right." She smooched him as she made for the bathroom. "Don't forget, I leave for London after work tonight."

"I know, that's why I stopped by, to say goodbye." He stopped her, pulling her close. "You've got this. No way Mitch will get promoted over you. You're way sexier. Just remember what we talked about." He looked at his phone buzzing away and frowned.

Her boyfriend was the team doctor for the Rangers and was even busier than she was, which was saying something.

"I remember. I'm going to take him down."

Ben grinned, showing off perfect white teeth. "You know, that's one of the things I like about you."

"What's that?"

"No drama. Sometimes you're like a guy but in a woman's body." He held up his hands. "Not that I have some kind of weird issues or anything; I'm just saying you don't get all wound up in the emotional stuff. You're practical and you're not clingy. I like that about you."

"Not like your ex, the beauty queen. What was she again, queen of green beans?"

He chuckled. "Queen of the sugar snap peas, five years in a row, the longest reign in town."

The gagging noises covered her shudder, making Ben chuckle.

"Thanks again for the hot chocolate. And for stopping by. I'll text you when I land, let you know how it goes. Better jump in the shower so I'm not late."

"The day you're late is the day the world ends."

"Funny." She kissed him, tasting the cinnamon on his lips. "Go have fun stitching up the players."

"Wouldn't have it any other way. We'll grab dinner when you get back. Celebrate your promotion."

While she finished getting ready, she'd been thinking about what Ben had said. Had she become too hard? Pushed aside her femininity so she could get ahead and be one of the guys? Mitch accused her of being as frozen as the snow blanketing the ground. At the time, she'd laughed and said better frozen than a puddle to be stomped in, but now she had to wonder. Where was the line between ambition and ball breaker?

During her commute this morning she used the precious time to read a few chapters of the novel she'd been reading for a month. Before college she'd read several books a week; now she was lucky if she read twelve in a year. A guy smelling like old cheese and cheap cologne passed by, making her throat close up. Gotta love the subway.

Over the past week she'd started jumping rope again after seeing a class at her gym using the rope to warm up. During college, it was like meditation, calming her mind from its normal state of flitting about like a butterfly on cocaine, but not today. She was really out of practice. After she got back in the groove, maybe the meditative feeling would return.

Blinking at the contrast between the dark subway and the stark brightness reflecting off the snow, she searched for a pair of sunnies in her bag as she stepped off the curb, jumping back as the swish of tires filled the air. A group of women on bicycles cycled past, wearing black leggings and nothing else but brightly colored paint. They looked like an abstract painting of a rainbow as they passed by, too quickly for her to read the protest signs they had tied to the bikes. Whatever. She'd seen women wearing less in nightclubs, and there was always some kind of protest going on, though the poor girls must be freezing.

Almost to the office, the shriek made her turn, but it was the accent that made her wince.

"Why I never. Harlan, did you see those gals? Wait till I tell Darlene. She'll never believe it. Tell me you got a picture. They must be colder than the devil in Siberia."

The man mumbled something Ashley couldn't hear as the woman's voice rang out across the street.

"Come on, let's get goin', I wanna be first in line."

The lilt, the dropped Gs. No matter how hard she tried, the past broke through the locked doors within and flooded her brain. Like a movie on fast forward, one blinking streetlight, cows in a pasture, empty shelves, and laundry flapping on the line in the sticky heat flashed in front of her eyes. Scowling at the tourists, Ashley huffed, weaving through the masses of people as if she'd been doing it her entire life instead of three short years.

"I can't escape. What is going on? Some kind of Southern special on visiting New York in the fall?" she grumbled under her breath as tourists stood in the middle of the escalator instead of standing to the right, so those on the left could actually walk past them and get to their offices on time. How could anyone in the civilized world not know that unwritten rule?

Maybe she needed to book a massage, because she was in a snit that even hot chocolate couldn't cure. The carpeted hallway muffled her steps, a few early risers working away. On the way to her office, she stopped to pick up her messages from the assistant she shared with two others. Of course the girl wasn't in yet; she usually rolled in around nine and took two hours for lunch.

The hedge fund was Ashley's first job out of college, and in the three years she'd been here, she'd worked her way up from an entry-level position to a junior executive at the age of twenty-three. She'd busted her butt, graduating both high school and college a year early, taking a full course load and ending with a double major in finance and economics. By the time she hit twenty-five, she planned to be a face on the org chart. But now the company was merging with a firm based in London so they could go global and be more competitive. With changes in leadership and her job on the line, there was no way she'd lose out to Mitch. She'd rather eat dirt and go crawling back to Georgia.

Her boss was older, still had the mentality that women should stay home and take care of the kids. Made it plain he thought she didn't belong, and she'd had to work twice as hard to prove otherwise.

Of course Mitch was already seated in Harry's office, the two of them laughing and joking. She pasted on a friendly smile as she strode into the immense corner office decorated in old-world elegance and oozing money.

"Ashley, nice of you to join us this morning." Mitch ran a hand through his hair. The kiss-up had obviously been here since dawn, beaten her in yet again. She'd have to step up her game; that was three times this month.

"Harry was telling me the news."

"News?"

He smirked at her. "Leadership has to tighten budgets. One junior executive has to go. Our little trip to London will decide who gets promoted and who gets canned."

She nodded at them both and lied through her teeth. "That's a great idea. Though wouldn't it make more sense to find something else for the loser? The firm puts a great deal of resources into training. Seems a shame to lose the knowledge."

Harry smiled at her as if she wasn't especially bright. "Women never want to make the hard choices. No, the loser will be packing up their desk and finding another job. I have goals to meet and I intend to exceed them. Leadership is watching."

"Works for me," Mitch said.

As Harry's assistant interrupted to tell him he had a call, Mitch and Ashley walked out together. In the hallway, he moved into her personal space. His breath was hot against her neck and she caught the scent of coffee and doughnuts.

"No one likes a manly woman. Don't you know by now? Harry likes the dumb model type. Look at all the assistants. Guess we both know who's going to be packing up when we get back."

Ashley stepped on his foot with her heel, pressing down hard.

"Damn, that hurt. You did that on purpose." Mitch scowled at her.

She paused in the doorway to her office. "You and Harry may be part of the good old boys' club, but I've worked hard to get where I am and there's no way you're taking this promotion from me. I've earned it."

"Game on, then. May the best man win."

She ignored him as she sat down and opened up the laptop, instead focusing on the day's tasks.

Before she knew it, the office was deserted, leaving Ashley and a few stragglers furiously typing away, blue light reflected on their faces. The sound of a vacuum droned from down the hall. She changed into a sweater dress and boots, hung her suit on the door, and left a note for her assistant to have it dry-cleaned while she was gone. Cashmere coat belted tight, chunky scarf in place, she was prepared to wait for a cab, but it was her night, as there was one in front of the building.

"JFK." Plenty of time to make the eleven o'clock flight.

Or so she thought.

"Doesn't it figure." She stared at the departures board in dismay as fellow travelers grumbled around her. In the time it took to get to the airport, the flight had been delayed. Hungry and irritable, she found a restaurant, only to discover everyone else had the same idea. Her dismay grew as she listened to the wait times at two other places. This was the downside of New York: everyone was used to getting what they wanted at all hours of the day and night. Not wanting fast food, she tried one last place where she could sit down, relax, and enjoy a glass of wine. As she was contemplating asking a group of businessmen if she could join them, a man managed to make himself heard above the din of the crowd. It was a cultured voice, one you knew came from the East Coast, with a lineage of horses, servants, a house on the Vineyard, and Ivy League schools. Mitch.

"Over here, dude. You can join me."

Suspicious, but grateful, she sat down, ignoring the *dude*. He called her dude or bro or fella all the time, trying to make some kind of stupid point. Usually she ignored him;

sometimes she responded at his level, calling him sugar, honey, girl, and chick. Immature, but it usually made her feel better.

"Thanks. Can you believe we've been delayed two hours?"

"There's a storm overseas. I had the office call ahead so they know we'll be arriving late."

The server stopped at their table, looking as frazzled as Ashley felt. After ordering, she sat back, people-watching. There were lots of business travelers and a few families with kids asleep at the table. Where were they all going?

Mitch talked about himself and what he was going to do with all the money from his promotion while she mainly nodded and enjoyed her dinner. Otherwise she was afraid she would end up screaming and having a full-blown tantrum in the middle of the restaurant. No, she would do what she always did. Work three times as hard as he did. At the end of the trip, she'd be the one laughing when Harry had to grudgingly concede she was the better person for the job. Mitch wiped his mouth and placed the white napkin to the side of his plate.

"Listen to me. I've been talking about myself all through dinner. So where are you from? I don't think I've ever asked."

"Buckhead."

Mitch's eyes rose. "Nice area. Had a friend at school from there. Maybe you know the family. The Winstons?"

She shook her head. "No. But then again, I was always studying. Didn't have much time to make friends."

He pursed his lips but didn't say anything, instead scratching his chin as he looked out over the restaurant. It was dimly lit and outrageously overpriced, but she was grateful for the warm meal and a chance to relax.

The cologne Mitch was wearing made her nose itch. Abruptly he turned to her and said, "You know, it's strange how much you remind me of a guy I knew at school."

"Really? Why strange?"

And just like that, she knew she'd made a mistake. Had seen that look on his face in meetings, the look of a shark ready to devour the helpless fish as it tried to swim away.

"The guy I knew had a huge chip on his shoulder. Scholarship student. Solid middle class; you know the type. Hated the kids with the latest phone, clothes, or sports car. He drove some old clunker we nicknamed the boat. Had a basic phone and generic laptop. Some old TV in his room. Think he was from some no-name town in the middle of nowhere. You know the type, always trying to pretend he was something he wasn't."

Ashley's insides felt as cold as the snow outside. Her nails dug into her palms so deeply she was surprised she hadn't drawn blood. But he couldn't see her hands under the table, and outwardly she plastered on her most serene smile and tilted her head up at him.

"I'm not sure what you mean, but I know the type. Every school has them, don't you think?"

He was interrupted from answering by the server bringing their check. Mitch reached for it. "I'll put this one on my expense report. You take the next one."

When she stood, the tablecloth caught on her belt, sending the wineglasses falling. Mitch caught the glasses before they hit the floor.

"Oops, tired, I guess. I'll see you on the plane. I've got a few things to catch up on. Thanks again for sharing your table." And without waiting for an answer, she briskly walked out of the restaurant, forcing herself not to run for the ladies' room and hide until it was time to board.

For one awful moment, she thought he'd found out her most shameful secret. But it was just Mitch being his horrible self, bluffing to see what she might confess. And there was no way Ashley would ever tell the truth about where she came from. Not to him or anyone else. Not ever.

Chapter Four

Why did he feel as if he'd spent the night sleeping on broken stone? Come to think on it, why was it so bloody cold? Had the fire gone out? Christian woke, the smell of rotting wood filling his nose, the taste of decay thick in his throat. A cloud of dust filled the hut when he stretched, his back cracking as he twisted. The leather flask was heavy in his hands as he tilted it to his mouth, letting the cold water quench his thirst.

"Pardon, my lord. Everyone has been searching for you." A small boy of no more than six winters stood in the doorway, shuffling his feet.

"You have been gone for two days." The boy looked hopeful as he blew his nose on his sleeve, the noise making Christian's horse snort.

"Might you return? The cook is making tarts, and the smell, it makes me hungry. Lord Ravenskirk said I might have one if I found you and brought you back. I'm one of the

best trackers, can find rabbits even in winter, everyone says
'tis so."

The look of hope and hunger on the boy's face made
Christian curse.

"What kind of tarts?"

The boy licked his lips, a lock of unruly black hair falling
over one eye, giving him the look of a rather small pirate
eyeing a vast treasure.

"Apple with cinnamon." He held a hand to his stomach as
if imagining the warm pastry filling his belly.

Grumbling under his breath, Christian swore again.

"Aye, I will return anon. You shall have your tart." The
boy's smile filled the room and banished the gloom from
Christian's soul. "You shall have two; tell my brother I said
such."

He was a Thornton. Thorntons always did their duty, and
for as long as Christian could remember, he wished to marry
and have babes to carry on the Thornton name. All of his
brothers were wed. 'Twas past time. Even if he had to knock
on every door in the realm, he would find another bride and
wed before year's end.

Resolved, he tossed the boy onto the horse and they rode
out as Christian hummed under his breath. The sky was a
muted gray, the smell of juniper and snow filled the air, and
he was grateful for the warmth of the scarf Lucy had made
for him. There was no wind; he could see Ravenskirk
reflected in the water surrounding the castle, making Henry's
home look twice its size.

The clatter of the horse's hooves on the bridge and the
sound of his and the boy's stomachs rumbling made such

noise that Christian was surprised the entire guard didn't turn out to see what army was invading.

The boy sniffed. "I smell the tarts."

"I do as well. We best make haste." Christian inhaled, his belly rumbling. In the future, if he ran away, he would pack victuals for the journey.

The boy jumped off the horse. "Shall I take him to the stables for you, my lord?"

"Aye, see to the horse, then fill your belly and bring me one of those tarts before my brother eats them all."

The lad took the reins, leading the horse away. Before Christian had gained the hall, a terrible scream rent the air, seeming to shake the very foundations of the keep as he drew his sword and ran. Inside the hall, there were no invaders, and his brothers were unharmed, pacing in front of the fire. William gaped at him whilst James looked to the stairs.

Christian looked about for the women. "Is aught amiss? Are we under attack?"

"The prodigal returns." Edward peered closely at him. "Why do you gasp like a fish out of water?"

"I heard screams, thought the women were in danger."

"Henry is in danger of losing his manly bits if the threats coming from Charlotte are to be believed." Edward rocked back on his heels. "With her in my army, I could take Scotland."

Another scream followed by a stream of cursing met Christian's ears, and he winced. "I didn't know Charlotte knew such words."

"She says it's fun to learn all the bad words." Henry gulped his wine and glanced toward the stairs.

Edward stroked his chin. "You were wrong, James. Christian looks like he spent the past two days in a barn, not enjoying the favors of a woman."

"Aye, so he does. Where have you been, dolt?"

"None of your concern. Can't a man spend a bit of time alone without you lot gossiping like old women?"

His eldest brother pursed his lips. "The lists. You will feel better after time in the lists." Edward rubbed his hands together. "Shall we go now?"

Christian scowled. "Not everything can be fixed by stomping about with a sword."

There was stunned silence.

"Truly? I find brawling in the mud does wonders." William smirked. "We should all have a go, see if your swordplay is as lacking as your ability to find a bride."

"Haven't you heard? I can find them; it's the wedding of them that's the problem." Christian rolled his eyes and turned his attention to Henry.

His brother, soon to be a father for the second time, was the same color as the clouds in the sky. His hands shook as he drank deeply from the goblet he was holding as if it had powers from faerie. "Have you seen Peter's monsters? How they terrorize the servants?"

William cuffed him on the ear. "If Lucy hears you speaking ill of our grandchildren, she will invite you out to the lists or poison your wine. Though, in truth, Peter would agree. I confess, we sometimes hide in the stables or the larder to escape the twins when they visit."

"Lads are easy," Henry said. "Give them a sword and send them to foster with a good family. But girls. And twins as well. They may only be four, but I would rather face a fire-breathing dragon than the two of them with mischief on their minds. Poor Peter." He shuddered.

"They're already beautiful," William said. "I'll have to kill every man that comes to woo them. I told my son his daughters are not to marry until they are two score, if ever." He grunted. "Did you hear what the angels did a fortnight ago? They put rotten eggs in all the guards' boots then sounded the alarm. Had been searching out old eggs and hiding them down in the cellar for months. When the guards put their boots on, the stench was dreadful." He leaned against the wall, crossing one booted foot in front of the other. "As all grandmothers, Lucy is blind to their faults. Thought they were clever to plan such a trick at their ages." He grinned. "I was rather proud of them, but don't tell my wife."

"Melinda thought it was amusing," James added. "Said when she was six she let a skunk into the car of a mean teacher; said she wasn't sure who was more alarmed, the skunk or the man. All the women look at those two savages and all they see are angels." He poured wine for them.

Robert entered the hall, pale and sweating. "James, I found your Emma with the boys. They were showing her how to throw a dirk. Saints, she's not yet two."

Christian clapped a hand over his mouth so he wouldn't laugh. Henry and John's sons might only be two years old, but they were more terrifying than the girls. When he had children they would be well mannered and well behaved.

James sprawled in the chair, legs stretched out in front of him. "Never too early for the lass to learn."

"Better not let Melinda hear you say such." Robert wiped his brow and poured a cup of the spiced wine.

James looked to the stairs as if worried his wife had somehow heard him, and this time Christian could not hold the laughter in.

"I will remind you of this moment when you have your own offspring."

He stopped laughing. Melinda could terrify the guard with a look. As his brothers had children, Christian watched them to see what kind of parents they might become. Anna and John let their son run free, while Charlotte and Henry believed in rules, which Christian found amusing. Though with their second child on the way, perchance his brother would not worry overmuch. Then again, what did he know? He didn't yet have babes. Or a wife.

As if she had heard Christian's thoughts, Charlotte let out another scream, causing Henry to spill his wine.

Christian paced the length of the hall, grateful everyone was too concerned with the coming babe to question him overmuch on where he had spent the past two days.

A sound on the stairs brought them to their feet as Melinda appeared, looking tired but full of joy.

"Congratulations, Henry. You have two beautiful girls."

Henry swayed, and would have ended up face first on the rug if James hadn't caught him. The rest of them were too stunned to move. More twins. Girls. Mayhap Christian had been too hasty in wanting children. He'd never thought he might have girls. What did one do with small females?

James pushed Henry down in the chair. "Put your head between your legs and breathe. Deep breaths."

The smell of whiskey filled the room. Robert inhaled deeply. "From Connor. Before he...left." He poured and passed a cup to Henry.

"Drink. You'll feel better."

Henry took two gulps before looking up at Melinda. "Did you say *two* girls?"

Melinda's joy filled the hall. And that quickly, Christian again wanted children, even twin girls. Surely they could not all be like Peter's daughters. He took a drink of Connor's whiskey, enjoying the smoky taste as the liquid pooled in his belly, filling him with warmth.

"Yes. Twins." She hugged Henry, her eyes meeting James, and something passed between them, bringing the loneliness back to Christian's heart.

"Ready to see your daughters?"

Henry nodded weakly. "Aye."

He allowed Melinda to lead him out of the hall.

"Well done, brother." Robert raised his cup.

John and Edward discreetly wiped their eyes as Henry passed by.

"Girls." Christian shuddered. "What does one do with girls?"

"Just wait, whelp. 'Twill be your time soon enough," William said before striding from the hall. "I'm for the lists. Who's with me?"

His entire family was gathered around the table. The ever-present loneliness Christian normally felt was replaced with joy at seeing Charlotte's new babes. It was decided to change the failed wedding feast into a celebration of new life. The hall was filled with sounds of merrymaking as the musicians played, voices carried through the hall as the men drank and jested, and his brothers teased him that it would soon be his time. In truth, he liked the noise. Winterforth was barren without the sound of children running about, stealing tarts from the kitchen. To have his family close was as much as he could ask for. He stretched his legs out under the table. 'Twas a good day.

Lucy draped one of her scarves around his neck and sat down beside him. "I'm sorry the kids played tug-of-war with the dogs and ruined your scarf. I made you another in blue to complement your eyes." She smelled of wine and wool, the silver of her hair shining like the moon in the candlelight.

"I'm awfully sorry about your betrothed. We all want you to be happy. So don't marry the next girl that comes along just because she's available. Make sure you care for her. I promise, the wait will be worth it." She brushed off her skirts as she stood, her gaze finding William. "After all, you'll be married the rest of your life. Might as well enjoy talking to her."

"I would be content to find one who would converse with me at all." Christian watched her go then turned his attention to the other women, shamelessly listening while pretending to enjoy the music as the women spoke of womanly matters.

The boy who'd found him in the hovel ran through the hall. Christian reached out and caught him. "Where are you off to?"

"He ate the tart I was saving for later, my lord." The boy glared at the retreating backside of another boy. One much larger.

Christian eyed the lad with a practiced eye. "He's bigger than you, and I've heard no one can best him among the stable boys."

The boy lifted his chin. There were crumbs on the front of his tunic, and they fell to the floor as he hopped about telling Christian what he would do to the boy when he caught him. Christian listened, making appropriate sounds until the lad was done.

"Might I offer a suggestion?"

The boy leaned forward to hear him above the noise in the hall.

"When he is in the privy, push him in, then run like hell."

The boy grinned. "He'll pound me, but 'twill be worth it."

"Aye. 'Tis good to stand up to those who are cruel to others." Christian hoped the boy wouldn't take too harsh a beating. Standing up for himself would show the bigger lad he would not back down. And some days that was all a man could ask.

Christian spent the evening talking to the lads about swords and battle and all the chivalrous duties a knight must perform. There was a warmth that filled the hall. Not from the fire, but from those within the walls of Ravenskirk.

Charlotte had changed Henry for the better. All of his

brothers were different. How might a wife change Christian?

Would she scream at him or be kind? Mayhap she would watch him in the lists and when he brawled in the hall with his brothers, cheering him on. As the years passed, what would it be like to have his family all together? It was important his brothers and their wives thought well of his bride. She would be part of the family he loved. All the women were beautiful, and he hoped his intended's visage would be pleasing. And when he made love to her, she would not turn away, but enjoy the act that would result in sons.

The merrymaking continued long into the night, and Christian was the last to retire to his chamber. As he stepped over men sleeping in the hall, he stopped to admire the painting Jennifer had done of Henry, Charlotte, and their son. Beside it was a painting of Ravenskirk Elizabeth had painted. He would ask them to paint his home and family when the time came.

The next morn Christian fussed over Charlotte and the babes, slapped Henry on the back, and filched the remaining tarts. He gave one to the lad who had tracked him to the hut. The boy had a black eye and split lip, but was otherwise unharmed.

"How did you fare?"

The boy grinned and sat on the stone wall facing the lists.

"You should have seen him. Splash. He flailed about, screaming like a wee girl. Didn't know he couldn't swim."

The boy hitched up his hose. "I fished 'em out and said don't ever cross me again."

"Good for you. Where is he now?"

"Skulking about." The lad held his nose. "In all me life I've never smelled such a stench."

The scarf Lucy had crocheted Christian was warm as the wind whipped through the courtyard. His family had come out to see him off. A lump formed in his throat at the thought of leaving them and traveling to Winterforth alone.

"Dust. I've dust in my eye."

Edward simply smiled and for once didn't say anything, which told Christian they all knew how he was feeling.

"Send word when you've arrived home."

Edward too wore a scarf, and as Christian looked around, he saw most of the people wearing Lucy's scarves and hats.

"Be careful going home. There have been odd happenings."

Robert sidled up to them. "Connor."

"Aye. I owe him my life for saving me from the Johnston hanging me." Edward grimaced.

"Do you know what's being said about our fearsome brother?" John embraced Christian, and he knew his brother understood his feelings. For John had been alone many years before rejoining the living.

James rocked back on his heels. "'Tis said you have powerful protection."

"From faeries," William added.

Edward scoffed. "Nonsense."

"Nay, brother." Robert spoke in a low voice so the lads in the lists wouldn't overhear them. Christian leaned forward too. He wasn't superstitious, but what had happened...

Robert continued, "You survived Maude trying to poison you. The Armstrong and Johnston failed to kill you, and were both killed in your stead, and now the Scots believe you to be immortal."

"I'd wondered why there hadn't been any raids of late." Edward stroked his chin. "I won't soon forget what happened."

"What are you lot whispering about like a bunch of gossips?" Melinda held out a parcel. "Charlotte sends her love. We all do. There's food for a se'nnight in there. Be careful." She kissed him on the cheek and turned to James. "I'll remind you of this day when you call me an interfering busybody, James Rivers."

"My shrew of a wife, how I love thee."

She blushed. "Flatterer."

"Go on," Henry said.

"It was an hour or so before dawn when we were attacked. One of the Scots had seen the thief's face and knew 'twas not me who burned." Edward's brother shivered. "The sky opened, the rain lashing us, then the lightning filled the sky. As I watched, Connor took an arrow through his hand, went down on one knee..." He wiped the sweat from his brow. "He vanished."

"Now the Scots believe you ate Connor for supper and that is why they could not find his body." William chuckled. "They may never vex you again. I shall remember this in case I needs strike terror in my enemies' hearts."

John gaped. "You would eat your enemy?"

"Nay." William scoffed. "But I would make sure no one ever found the body so they thought I did."

"Do you think the same thing happened to Connor as did your wives?" Christian paled at the thought of Connor finding himself facing the Romans.

"Mayhap. We will never know." Henry pulled Christian into an embrace. "What an adventure he must be having. I will miss you, brother."

Christian bade each one goodbye—his throat pained him so that he did not trust himself to speak without bawling like a babe.

Before he rode out of the gates, a commotion sounded, the dogs running out of the keep as if chased by demons from hell. Each dog was dyed a different color. One yellow, one green, and one a rather sickly shade of blue. The boys ran after them as fast as their small, chubby legs would carry them. Jennifer chased after them brandishing one of her paintbrushes.

"You little monsters, you used all of my paint."

She came to a stop and blew the hair out of her face before turning to the group. "Did you see what they did? They painted the dogs."

He couldn't hold it in: Christian threw back his head and laughed as William and John narrowed their eyes.

"Your time is coming," John said.

Elizabeth clapped a hand over her mouth, but the giggles escaped. "Maybe they were just trying to help you."

Jennifer waved the paintbrush at her. "If you want me to make more paint for you, you'll quit laughing, otherwise you're out of luck."

Elizabeth hugged her sister-in-law. "You know I'm only teasing."

"I know. But it makes me mad." Jennifer huffed, a bit red in the face, the scent of her paints following she and Elizabeth wherever they went.

Halfheartedly, she called after them, "You better run, you little monsters. I'm giving your slice of pie to the dogs."

The boys were wise enough to remain quiet.

As he rode out across the bridge, Christian thought of Winterforth filled with the sound of laughter, the loneliness banished for good. With one last look at Ravenskirk, he had the feeling the next time he was here, his life would be irrevocably changed.

Chapter Five

Careful not to bang into anyone with her carry-on, the sight of slicked-back blond hair had Ashley searching for a way to cross the aisle to avoid *him*.

"Tell me you're not stuck in the back with the other cows?"

Nope. Too late.

"Of course you upgraded to first. I'm in business."

Mitch looked like he'd gotten a good whiff of garbage on a hot summer day.

"Bad enough. Listen, Ash, I've already taken care of renting a car, so you can catch a ride with me when we land. We'll need to get checked in at the hotel and changed for the costume party. It's a bit of a drive out to the country. Some moldy old estate; probably reeks of dust and old rugs. We're to arrive dressed."

"What do you mean a costume party?" Her fingers and

toes went numb. "You said it was a cocktail party. What kind of costume party?"

"Oh, didn't you know? Guess Harry didn't tell you. It's a medieval costume party. Havers loves the era, and we're to arrive dressed." He looked her up and down. "My assistant called ahead to let them know we're running late, but assured them we'd make it to the party by the end of cocktails at the latest. I don't know why we couldn't get dressed there, since we're staying overnight. I hear our new boss is brilliant with numbers but crazy—oh, excuse me, eccentric."

She pressed her lips together, rolling her shoulders to ease the knots. Now she knew why he'd offered to share his car: he'd sabotage her, make sure she didn't have a costume, and put himself one step closer to winning. *Payback's a bitch, Mitch.*

"No, Harry didn't tell me. Appreciate the offer, but I'll grab a cab, since now I need to find a costume."

"Good luck." He glanced at his watch. "We won't land until one, and it's at least a two-hour drive to the estate, so by my estimation, you'll have a max of three hours to find a dress and change in order to leave on time...and we all know how important it is for you to be on time. I'll be looking forward to seeing what you come up with, and don't worry, I'll let Havers know you're running late."

He flicked a glance behind her. "Better move on. You're holding up the line."

"See you there." Ashley gritted her teeth and smiled so she wouldn't smack him and get thrown off the plane. The suitcase banged into his seat, and he yelped as the drink splattered on his sleeve. Served him right.

"Cardiff, Wales. What do you mean we're landing in Wales?"

The man seated next to her shrugged at the announcement from the cockpit. Ashley felt the hysteria rising, threatening to spill over and make her run screaming down the aisle.

A severe storm had shut down Heathrow, diverting them to Wales, where there was another storm, but apparently not so bad they couldn't land. It was supposed to clear in a few hours. The Wi-Fi on the plane didn't work, some kind of mechanical issue, so she had to wait until she landed to search out a dress for tonight.

By the number of people making use of the little bags behind their seats and the stench filling the cabin, she should have known there would be a problem. Only an iron will had kept her from barfing along with most of the passengers as the turbulence grew worse.

The man next to her closed his eyes, gripping the armrest, his lips moving over and over. Finally the announcement came they were landing. The passengers couldn't get off the smelly plane fast enough. Stale air, vomit, and peanuts—it was revolting.

After she cleared customs, Ashley tried to call Mitch. It was time to put her dislike of him aside. They could ride together, and she'd call shops on the way for a costume to wear to the party. London would have lots of shops with dresses, right? Surely an hour would be enough time to find a dress? She'd wear it out of the store and make it in time for dinner. But he was nowhere to be found. Not at the rental counter, and definitely not answering his phone.

She spoke to the woman behind the rental counter.

"Wait, you don't have any cars? I'll take anything, except a motorcycle. Don't know how to ride one of those." When she leaned on the counter, her palms encountered something sticky. Gross. She rummaged in her bag for a tissue and discreetly wiped down the area.

The sound of the woman's fingers on the keyboard were like tapping against a window. Each time she typed, Ashley swore she smelled apples. Was it hand lotion?

"No, I'm terribly sorry. With the storm and the additional passengers from London, we've had everyone wanting a car today."

She tried Mitch again. No answer. Why did she have the feeling he'd done this on purpose? He must be laughing, knowing she would be stuck in Wales while he drove to London, probably had his assistant book the car as soon as they touched down while she'd been too busy thinking about the damn dress. By the time she arrived, Mitch would have already kissed up to Mr. Havers and would be the one taking home the promotion. She'd be the one packing up the sad little cardboard box while her coworkers whispered and wore sad fake smiles on their faces.

No. This was not happening. She'd worked too hard, sacrificed too much to give up now. A pit stop in the ladies' room where she touched up her makeup and put her hair up in a ponytail, and Ashley was ready to do battle.

Though an hour later she was forced to concede defeat. There was a problem with the train: it was delayed until late afternoon. The cabs and limos were gone, already spoken for, and she hadn't had any luck getting a boat, either. The man on the phone thought she was joking when she asked about helicopters, and hung up on her. As she slumped in a chair, drinking a bottle of sparkling water, the smell of pine needles made her nose itch.

"Heard you need a ride to London."

The guy was dressed in jeans and a sweater with his hair pulled back in a ponytail. He gestured to the door. "My mum works for the rental company. Said I was to find the nice American and see if she wanted the car that just came in."

The water shot out of the bottle as she squeezed it hard. "Oops. Yes, I want the car. Thank you, you've saved my job."

"Don't know about all that. Come along before there's a stampede." He looked back at her. "She said you were the only one who didn't yell at her."

"Why would I? It's not her fault the sky is falling. Unless she's Mother Nature and she works at a rental car company in an airport for fun."

The guy pretended to think about it. "Some days I think she could be Mother Nature. When she's mad, I take myself off to the pub until she calms down a bit."

"I'm sure that makes her happy."

The guy left her at the counter, and after filling out the

forms, she was in possession of the last rental car in all of Wales, for all she knew. Let Mitch think he'd won. On the way, she'd call the hotel and have them hold her room, then she'd call costume shops, and once she arrived in London, she'd skip the hotel, go straight to the shop, wear the dress out, and drive as fast as she could out to the country estate of Mr. Havers.

It was a little after two now, with the three and a half hours there, a half-hour at the shop, and two to the estate... She'd never make it. That would put her there at eight tonight if nothing went wrong and she floored it all the way.

She sat in the car, adjusting the mirrors, and made the call. "Dot, it's Ashley—"

"I heard you had to land in Wales. How's the weather?"

She tapped her foot. "Listen, I need Mr. Havers' number. I'm running late."

There was silence. "You're running late? Is the world ending?"

"Funny, Dot. The number."

She waited until her assistant came back on the line with the number.

"Thank you. Could you call shops between Wales and the estate, as well as London, and see if you can find me a medieval dress? Maybe I can make the after-dinner drinks."

"Okay, that's a lot of calls, but I'll see what I can find online first. Dinner isn't until eight—Mr. Havers eats late—so as long as you arrive by ten or eleven at the very latest, I think you'll be fine."

Ashley hung up and dialed the estate, where she spoke to the butler or somebody who said they would inform her new boss. He was aware of the weather and understood. Flexing her hand to get the blood flowing again, she punched the air. "Yes!"

With a cushion of a couple of hours, she'd make it no problem. Impressed by her charm and good looks, Mr. Havers would offer her the promotion on the spot, and Mitch would be the one walking briskly out of the building, carrying the pathetic box.

A horn honked and she waved. "Sorry. American here. Not used to driving on the left."

Okay, so the guy couldn't hear her, but it made her feel better to say something. For the next hour, she paid attention to the road and focused on staying on the left. Before she left for the trip, Dot had asked her about driving on the left, couldn't understand why everyone didn't drive on the right. Ashley had dredged up some obscure bit of knowledge and told her it was because America was such a young country compared to Europe. Her assistant was sweet but not that bright, and blinked at her.

"What do you mean?"

"In the past, in a feudal and violent society, pretty much everybody traveled on the left because it was sensible. Think about it. Most people were right-handed, and swordsmen preferred to keep to the left so their right arm was closer to an opponent and their sword." And that was the extent of her medieval knowledge. Not like she needed to know anything else; she worked in finance, not at a museum or historic site. Always forward, never back. That was her mantra.

The girl had nodded. "So we drive on the right because we never cared about all that silly stuff."

"Something like that." Ashley went into her office to gather up a few more files. Dot was incredibly nice, but sometimes Ashley wondered how the girl managed to get the job. Her company wasn't known for hiring those with less-than-average intelligence. And then she remembered someone saying that Dot had a cousin high up in the firm, which explained a lot. Or maybe Mitch was right and Harry only hired bimbos.

A half-hour later, Dot called. "I couldn't find anything, and I'm late for my date, so just show up as you are and smile. It will all work out."

And that was Dot. Sweet and completely out of touch with the real world. "Thanks for trying."

With a little under two and half hours to go until she arrived in London, Ashley wasn't conceding defeat yet. She used the voice assistant on the phone, furiously calling shops. By the fifth call, she'd hit pay dirt. The man promised to hold the two dresses he described and stay open for her. Both sounded perfect for a medieval night in the countryside. Mr. Havers was a bit obsessed with the time period, and she wished she'd had more time to review history so she could contribute something interesting to the after-dinner conversation.

Ashley firmly believed in visualizing her goals and imagining where she would be in five years. The only thing looking back was good for was regret, and she was not going there. Regret didn't help anyone. And since it didn't serve a purpose, she refused to indulge.

As the road curved and she went through yet another small town, Ashley spotted a pub. The hollow feeling in her stomach had gotten worse as she drove. She needed to eat, especially since she wouldn't get anything until morning if she didn't make dinner. With a look at her watch, she put the turn signal on. Mitch would be doing whatever he could to annoy her tonight, so she couldn't afford to be cranky. She'd have to take the precious half-hour and eat. Stopping would put her to the party by eight thirty. She'd eat fast.

The interior was dim, with a few locals at the bar. There was a couple heads bent, whispering to each other, and she quickly averted her eyes. On the other side of the pub was a table of guys talking loudly, and at another table, a family of four. Ashley chose a table next to the family. She ordered at the bar and sat down, scrolling through the notes on her tablet.

The aroma of freshly baked bread wafting up from the plate made her drool as she carried the meal to the table. The rolls were perfect. Crisp and crunchy on the outside and light and fluffy on the inside. It would be easy to eat an entire plate of those little bits of heaven. The stew was just as delicious, the vegetables done perfectly and the sauce rich and filling.

As she quickly ate, she looked around the pub, trying to avoid the far left corner. But no matter how hard she tried, her eyes kept straying to the couple. There was something about the way he looked at her, the softness in his eyes, that made her flinch.

For as long as she could remember, relationships had been hard for her. All around her, friends paired off, broke up, and found someone new. While she went ages and ages before she found anyone. Everyone made it seem so easy, but to her it was exhausting. Between work and staying fit, and making sure she was on track to meet her five-year plan, Ashley had given up on dating.

And then she met Ben. Her company had season tickets to the Rangers, and she'd always liked hockey. Had thought perhaps if people vented their frustrations on the ice, maybe everyone would get along better. At one of the games, a puck sailed over the glass and hit the man beside her. She stayed with him until the medical personnel arrived. While she was cleaning herself up, she met Ben, the team doctor. He'd been the only guy brave enough in a long time to breach her porcupine exterior, so when he asked her out, she said yes. They'd been dating for the past few months.

He was attractive, successful, and sometimes she wondered what he saw in her. Ashley knew she came off as prickly and standoffish, but they seemed to get along well enough. Though she still found herself thinking about their relationship, wondering if there was anything she could do to make it easier, and why it always felt like work.

The sound of a horse approaching had Christian unsheathing his sword. He put the blade back in its sheath when he recognized the figure.

Edward reined in the horse, sending mud flying as he

wiped the sweat from his brow.

"A messenger arrived not long after you left. Melinda and James met a wealthy merchant at the last market day. They did not want to say anything until it was decided. The girl's father has agreed to the match." Edward dismounted and left the horse to graze.

Christian gaped at his brother as he wiped mud from his cheek. It smelled of decay and earth. "What girl?"

"Her father is a merchant, so she is not a noble, though I think you do not care as long as she has all of her teeth." Edward waved a hand. "All that is of consequence is she has said she will plight her troth to you."

"Do they know what is said about me?"

"Her father knows, but for a great deal of gold he has agreed for her to wed you anyway. He is desperate to raise their station and see his daughter make a good match. He promised his wife on her deathbed."

"And you said I would pay."

His brother slapped him on the shoulder. "Aye. What good is gold if you do not spend it? You would give all your gold to find a wife, would you not?"

Instead of answering, Christian scowled. It was true, but he did not like to hear his brother make him sound like a boy pining after his first love, the evil ogre hiding alone in his castle waiting for his bride. 'Twas pitiful.

"You are to marry before Yule. The girl will be delivered to Winterforth in six weeks. We will all travel for the wedding. Best stock the larder; you know how our brothers eat and drink."

Christian handed Edward the leather flask. "Drink. You

sound like a fish pulled from the sea."

"Have you nothing to say, dolt?"

"Nay, I will not believe 'tis so until we stand in the chapel and say the vows."

"As you wish. You have lost many brides, but you should not let this worry you overmuch. This will be the girl. You will be married and she will bear you a son before the next year is done, putting all the rumors to rest."

His brother handed back the flask, wiping his mouth with the back of his hand. The smell of ale filled the air.

Christian was unconvinced. "We shall see."

"Shall I ride with you to Winterforth? You should not be without your guard."

"Nay, I'm meeting them in a few days. 'Twill be fine. You worry overmuch." He did not tell Edward he had one stop to make first. One that did not involve his guards or his meddlesome brothers. For if he was caught…

Chapter Six

Ashley had finished congratulating herself on keeping left when she came upon a scene straight out of a chocolate-induced nightmare.

On her right, a monkey swung from the trees. To the left, a zebra ran through the field, and was that...? It couldn't be. Oh yes it was: a tiger ran in front of the car and bounded after the zebra. Tires squealed as she slammed on the brakes, coming to a stop inches from a deep ditch. Fingers crossed, she hoped the zebra would get away.

Up ahead lay an overturned truck. People were running around checking the remaining cages and looking helplessly up at the monkey. Too stunned to laugh, she slowed down as a policeman motioned her to stop.

"The highway's closed while we catch the animals, miss. Turn right up ahead then take a left past the old church, a right past the twisted tree, and another right past the bridge.

Then you'll see signs to get back on the motorway."

"Got it. Good luck catching them." She mentally recited the directions as she made the turn up ahead, though she hoped the animals might find a place to live in the countryside where they wouldn't bother anyone. A remnant hope left over from all the books she'd read as a kid. The books with talking animals were her favorites. The world was changing. Would a zoo be the only place to see wild animals in the next twenty or thirty years? She hoped not.

A half-hour later as the roads narrowed until she was on what looked like an overgrown sidewalk, she had to concede she was lost and had missed a turn along the way. The map on the phone took over, and as she followed the directions, she thought about her presentation at the London office later this week. It had to go well.

Busy thinking about the graphs and charts she needed to update, Ashley frowned. The phone hadn't said anything for ages, the sun had set, and a glance at the screen told her it was five o'clock. She should have been close to London by now. What happened?

There was a place up ahead to fill up, so she pulled over and looked at the directions. This was not her day. Somehow she must've incorrectly entered the address. So she put it in again. After paying for the gas and a water, she was on the way.

According to the navigation, another hour and a half to London. That would put her at the party at nine thirty—pushing it but still doable. She was humming along to the radio, following the turns, when the voice said, "You have arrived at your destination. Your destination is on the left."

"What the hell?" The phone showed the end of the journey, but that couldn't be right. She'd gone from the road to stone, and now to a narrow, grassy road that looked like nothing more than a dirt path up ahead. There had to be a place to turn around up ahead—no way she could manage it here—so she kept going and found herself driving on grass again when the road abruptly ended.

She got out of the car to stare through the growing darkness at the surrounding countryside.

"Where the hell am I?"

"Having a spot of trouble?"

Ashley's mouth fell open at the sight the car headlights illuminated. It was a guy—no, make that a model—on an actual horse. What was a model doing cavorting about the countryside? Because something about him made *cavorting* the only appropriate word to fit, with his long black hair, perfect dimples in his chin and cheeks, and, oh, let's not forget the eyes so blue they looked fake. He wore a pair of old jeans, a sweater, and what she guessed was a Barbour jacket. Ben had one just like it. She rubbed her eyes in case she was hallucinating. Nope. He was still there. It was as if she'd wandered into a shoot for a magazine.

"There was a detour on the highway and I got turned around." She held up the phone. "I think my maps app played a trick on me. I don't suppose I'm going to find London over that next hill, am I?"

The model blinked at her. "London? You are lost. That must have been some kind of crazy wrong turn. You're not even in the right country. This is Wales."

No, no, no. This wouldn't do. "You have got to be kidding

me. There's no way I'm in Wales. I left Wales this morning."

She was so busy picturing herself packing up her office and sitting alone in her apartment eating cheesecake day and night that it took a moment to realize he was talking to her.

"Miss?"

"Sorry?" Ashley snapped out of it. "Okay, forget London. This is where I have to be by eleven at the very latest tonight." She showed him the address.

"I know the place. Did a shoot out there last month. It's in the countryside; you've got a good long drive ahead."

An odd shaky feeling started in her legs, moving up to her arms, and sounds were muffled like she had cotton in her ears. His voice sounded like it was coming from a cartoon.

Don't panic. You've got this. There was no way she was losing out on her promotion all because the maps app was possessed.

"Is there any shopping nearby? Or a Halloween store? I need a medieval-style dress for a costume party tonight. It's really important."

The guy, who was way too good-looking to be human, stuck his tongue in the corner of his mouth as he thought about her question. As she was about to scream, his face brightened.

"Old Mary makes costumes for the theater company. I'm sure she'll have something. I'll take you."

"Won't the car spook your horse?"

"Leave it here. You can ride with me. It will be faster, and I'll bring you right back."

"On that? In the dark?"

He looked offended. "She isn't a *that,* and she knows her

way." He patted the horse and leaned down to whisper in the animal's ear. "Don't mind her. She's just a mean old Yank.

"The roads between here and the village are narrow, some barely wide enough for the horse. Your car won't fit."

Ashley eyed the horse.

"Don't worry; she won't bite." Then he winked at her. "Unless you keep offending her."

With another glance at her watch, a sigh escaped. "All right. But we have to hurry."

He dismounted and lifted her up as if she weighed nothing. Then he climbed up behind her, put one arm around her waist, making her flinch, and took the reins.

"It's just so you won't fall off. You're not my type."

She stiffened in the saddle. "I knew that."

He chuckled and made some kind of clucking noise to make the horse go forward.

Could they go any slower? At this rate, she'd have wrinkles by the time they made it to the village. The horse stepped over a branch, and Ashley looked down for the twentieth time, the dark playing tricks on her. When she first saw the horse it didn't seem that high up, but now, riding on its back, it seemed a really long way to the ground if she fell.

The smell was back. She sniffed. Was it coming from the

horse or the saddle or both? Another sniff told her it was both, though it was probably normal animal smells. Ugh, it was worse than some of the subway stations in the city. The model's cologne mixed with the horse smell, making her slightly nauseated. Figured she was wearing her sweater dress and boots, the ones that made her feel invincible. Too bad they weren't working on this trip.

It was a quaint town straight out of an old movie. The guy, whose name she still didn't know, rode to the end of the street, turned left, and stopped in front of a hobbit-sized house sitting slightly apart from its neighbors, windows glowing, and smoke coming from the chimney. Ashley had the oddest feeling that a witch lived inside.

When he lifted her off the horse, she lost her balance. Thank goodness he caught her before she hit the ground.

"You've never ridden before." He said it like it was some terrible thing, like she'd never used a fork to eat with, so it took considerable willpower not to give him the finger.

"No. I live in New York City. We use cars, buses, cabs, or the subway for transportation. Not horses."

The guy winced. "All that concrete and steel, no fresh air. How do you stand it?"

"I could ask you the same thing."

The door to the tiny house swung open and a tiny lady with blue hair peered out before she turned around to push a dog back inside. She was dressed in a pink velour tracksuit with the words *sexy grandma* across her butt, making Ashley grin.

"Who do we have here, Douglas?"

The guy, apparently named Douglas, hugged the woman,

kissing her wrinkled cheek. The scent of lavender drifted toward Ashley, tickling her nose.

"Found her up on the old sheep path. She'd taken a wrong turn, thought she was in England, says she needs a dress for a party tonight."

The woman pursed her lips. "Come along inside and we'll fix you up."

It had taken Christian ten days to journey from Ravenskirk to the tavern in Wales where he would meet his partner. He had not told his brother the truth, for his men were not meeting him along the way. Two of his most trusted guards were already in Wales, staying at the tavern where Christian would transact his business. What he was about to do was between the three of them, and no one else would know.

Meeting a smuggler would be frowned upon by his family —well, perchance not John, since he had been the bandit of the wood, but still, 'twas a risk, and Christian did not want to expose his family to danger.

He had his reasons. Two of them. One was he needed gold to continue his other labors, and two, he chafed at the tax collected on his wool. Winterforth produced high-quality wool, known throughout the realm. This summer he had added to his flock, and 'twas now four thousand strong. Every year the wool was taken to Westminster to be sold, and every year he grew angrier and angrier at the amount of taxes collected.

From Westminster the wool was sent to Flanders and Italy—'twas the way things were done. Then a few months ago, Christian was in a tavern when a brawl broke out, and a man ended up with his head split nearly in two. Christian aided the man, only to find out later he was a smuggler, and apparently a very good one.

The man knew Christian was a Thornton, had seen the quality of wool from Winterforth, and proposed a plan. Christian thought it bold and daring, and if it worked, it would allow him to do more for others in need.

The smuggler had a great many connections. It was decided he would come to Winterforth up the river by barge, collect the wool Christian had held back from this summer, and take it where it would be loaded onto boats and sold without any taxes paid. He would continue to sell a portion at Westminster to avoid questions, but in time he hoped to sell the bulk through the smuggler.

If he was found out, it would shame his family, and after all the Thorntons had been through, he wanted to shield them from his doings.

This was how he found himself creeping along like a common thief in the night as he went to meet the man. The tavern was questionable, the kind of establishment where Christian might find his horse missing at the end of the night, so he flipped the boy an extra coin.

"See to it he is well cared for and there will be another

coin for you when I depart."

The boy bobbed his head. "As you say, my lord."

During his journey, Christian had changed into his oldest hose and tunic so as not to draw attention to himself. He frowned at the sword the boy likely recognized was that of a knight or a lord. From his experience, boys noticed everything, whilst men saw what they wished, so he would present himself as a well-to-do merchant. Lord Winterforth was, as far as Christian was concerned, at home in his keep.

The tavern was smoky, the smell of ale overlaid with burned cooking and unwashed bodies filling the air. With so many men packed into the small room, the heat was intolerable. Christian breathed shallowly through his mouth as he made his way to the corner, where he saw the man sitting in shadow.

For a rather infamous smuggler, the man had a fitting name. Morien. Meaning sea-born. It agreed with his dark hair and even darker eyes.

"Were you followed?"

Christian shook his head. "Nay. I was most careful."

He sat down, stretching his legs beneath the scarred table. A serving wench sashayed over, eager to do Morien's bidding. He patted her on the rump as she left, winking at them both.

"The ale is good, the food edible."

When the food and drink arrived, Christian thought Morien had been rather generous in his pronouncement. For while the ale was drinkable, 'twas watered down, the bread was full of tiny rocks, and the stew was greasy. Somehow he choked it down, not willing to draw attention to himself, as

LAST KNIGHT   68

the other patrons seemed to take no issue with what they were shoveling into their mouths.

"You are certain you will not be discovered?"

Morien leaned back into the corner of the wall so only his nose and mouth were visible in the light, giving him the appearance of a spirit.

"I've had men watching the river for a month. There is one day each week 'tis not safe, but the rest will be fine if we go at night, as I have planned. But what of the guards at Winterforth?"

"The two men I brought with me will guard the walls on that side of the river. The rest will not know what we are doing."

"Secrets rarely stay so. Be prepared." Morien's gaze darted to the right. "I see the one with light hair by the fire with the saucy wench on his lap." Then he looked over Christian's shoulder. "The other is wagering; his blade gives him away. As does yours. No wealthy merchant would have such a fine sword. Only a noble such as yourself."

"We will not draw attention to ourselves, and my men can be trusted. I do not wish anyone in Winterforth to be in danger from what I am doing, so I will keep this from them as long as I can."

Morien studied Christian. "Why did you help me? You could have left me to die. Most would have."

"'Twas five against one, and whilst those odds might be fine for a Thornton, you looked as if you were not ready to die that night. I thought you could use a man at your back." The corner of his mouth twitched.

Morien picked his teeth. "Aye, you may be right. Still, you

knew who I was and yet you aided me."

"I could not leave you to die. Since we spoke, I have thought much on your plan."

"Not that I care, but what will you do with all this gold? Is it true what they say?"

"What's that?"

Morien leaned forward in the light so Christian could see his eyes. "That you can never have enough gold?"

Christian drained his cup. "Many would say such. I have uses in mind for the gold."

He realized he had said too much, for Morien's look turned speculative before a feral grin broke out across his face.

"'Tis you."

Christian pretended not to know what the smuggler meant.

"You are the one who aids those in need. They speak of you throughout London. A poor widow finds the money she needs to pay her rent or put food on the table. A young boy finds he has been apprenticed to learn a trade; a pretty girl is married not to the old lecher but someone more appropriate. All those are you."

Christian met his gaze. "As you trust me to keep your secrets, I must trust you to keep mine."

Morien gazed at him for a bit longer and then nodded. "You have my word. Will you take the word of a smuggler?"

"Nay, not of the smuggler but of the man." Christian held out a hand. They shook, and he knew Morien would not tell others of his deeds. He would be able to aid so many. What was the use of having money if one could not do with it as one pleased?

Chapter Seven

"I can't thank you enough, Mary. How funny is it that a medieval dress is going to save a present-day job?"

"We have to work twice as hard in a man's world to be taken seriously, don't we? The trick is not to let them know we know we're smarter." Mary winked at Ashley.

The dress was beautiful. It reminded her of a long vest over a maxi dress. There was a linen embroidered underdress called a shift, then the gown, and what she thought of as a vest was the surcoat. She'd only seen embroidery like this in a museum or on haute couture. All around the neck, sleeves, and hem were a riot of flowers and leaves. The surcoat was made out of bronze velvet, and embroidered within an inch of its life with gold metallic thread. The gown had a corset built in, so she didn't have to wear a bra. There was also a hidden zipper placed so she could reach it, to get in and out of the dress by herself. As she smoothed her hands down the dress, she felt an opening.

"Pockets. Perfect. I can keep my phone with me."

"They wouldn't have been invented in the early 1400s, but all my customers want them, so I put them in. And really, what does it matter? Not like you're going to the past." Mary made a small adjustment to the ornate belt at her waist and stood back to take in her work. "No one wore underwear then, if you're wanting to get in the spirit of the party," she said with a wink.

Ashley folded her undies and bra and stuffed them in her bag, along with the sweater dress she'd been wearing when she arrived.

"Why not?" She caught sight of her reflection, and the woman staring back at her was pretty. Her hair had been braided with tiny pearls woven in the strands, making her feel like a supermodel.

She took a step forward, watching the thread shimmer. "I don't know how women used to walk. This is heavy. Guess that's why they didn't have to work out."

"Are you sure you don't want the shoes?"

Ashley pulled the dress up, showing off her boots. "Nope. These are my favorite boots. I can run if I need to, and it's not like anyone will notice, since the dress goes to the floor. I once ran ten blocks in these to make a meeting on time. They're my version of armor."

There was a knock on the door, and Douglas the model came in. "Wow, you are smoking hot."

He stared at her from her feet to her head, stopping at her chest for a minute too long. There was rather a bit of cleavage on display. When in the theater, one must look ravishing, was Mary's answer.

"Thank you, Douglas." Ashley turned to Mary. "I don't know how to thank you. The work on this must have taken a thousand hours. Are you sure I paid you enough?" Her coat looked ridiculous over the dress, but it was only for the ride back to the car. She hoped there would be valet parking at the party so she could leave her coat off to make her entrance.

"You paid plenty, love. I charged you the rush rate. The dress was done—just needed a nip here and a tuck there. The actress I made it for took a role in a futuristic film, so she didn't need it." Mary grinned. "You best get going if you want to make it to the party on time. Can't have you turning into a pumpkin and let that rat you work with win, now can we?"

"Absolutely." On impulse, Ashley hugged the woman goodbye, feeling like she was hugging a tiny doll, though a doll made of fire and steel with a dash of humor thrown in for good measure. Outside, she was relieved the horse wasn't tied to the gate.

Douglas must have read her mind.

"I brought the bike so you wouldn't get hair on the dress. If you tuck your skirts up and hold them, you should be fine. It isn't far, and I've taken a few of the actresses in similar dresses between the theater and Mary's house."

While she'd been on the back of a motorcycle before, she hadn't had so much dress to manage. Careful not to crease the dress, she pulled it around her then took the scarf from her coat pocket and covered her hair.

"I'm ready. Don't go too fast or you'll mess up my hair." She put her arms around him; the guy had a torso to rival a superhero.

"I know how you women are about your hair. Don't worry about a thing, it'll be grand."

He kept his word as he drove them through the tiny pathways, back to the rental car. Practically hopping off the bike, she held out a hand.

"You've been my knight in shining armor. Thank you, kind sir."

He opened the compartment on the side of the bike, coming out with a flashlight and paper bag, which he handed her.

"You're welcome. Figured you'd be hungry, so I stopped by the pub and picked you up something to eat on the way."

"Probably won't get a bite until morning, so I really appreciate it, thanks. Now remind me which way to go. I don't trust my phone anymore."

The flashlight illuminated a napkin with what looked like a hand-drawn map.

"It's really easy: turn around and take the first right, and then follow my map, which bypasses London. Once you get back on the motorway you can pick up speed, and you should make it before the clock strikes twelve. Just don't lose your glass slipper. I've given you a shortcut, should save you about half an hour, maybe a bit more. Put you there around ten thirty or eleven."

He waved as he rode off, and with a frown at her watch, she climbed in the car, determined to make it and show off the amazing dress.

The first couple of turns went fine, but then she came to an area that was supposed to look like a twisted fork. All she saw was a turn left or right. Debating for a moment, she took a left and kept going. After driving around in what she thought was a giant circle, she realized she was lost. Again. Drop her anywhere in the city and she could find her way, but here? It was as if fate was conspiring against her at every turn.

A wooden sign leaned to the right. The words *Ruins ahead* had been hastily painted on, as if some enterprising farmer was trying to entice lost tourists to stop. Dubiously eyeing a wooden bridge that looked a million years old, she held her breath as she drove over it, and then parked under a tree that looked as old as the bridge. Ashley stopped the car, caught the water bottle with her sleeve, and watched in horror as the water turned the napkin to mush, the black words blurring into a charcoal mess.

"Damn it!" Somewhere there had to be a road sign. *Think. What were the next few turns?* She got out of the car, using the flashlight on her phone to look around, holding the possessed phone above her head, trying to get a signal. After stepping in two mud puddles, she swore until she ran out of curse words.

"I hate it when technology fails."

The wind kicked up, the clouds hiding the moon. There was a hill up ahead. Maybe if she walked to the top she could see the surrounding area. With the dress held high so it wouldn't get dirty, she carefully made her way up the hill. The boots had cost a fortune, but were worth every penny. The Welsh countryside might throw mud on her, but she was getting out of this country if it was the last thing she did.

At the top of the hill, she turned in a circle, but there was only countryside and more countryside in every direction. In vain she looked for a sign, even using the camera on her phone to zoom in, but it was too dark. Today was not her day. Ignoring the warning signs, she hiked up the ruins to see if she could get at least one bar on the useless phone.

Startled by a sound like two cars colliding at high speed, she spun around. But there weren't any cars. For that matter, no trains or people or other big vehicles that might have been responsible for the noise.

Funny, it almost sounded like a battle like in the video games Mitch plays when he thinks no one is around. The stress of being late was making her imagine things.

The scene in front of her had turned gray. Fog was rolling in and quickly. The sound of thunder made her jump, and lightning flashed across the night sky.

Great—you don't do camping, no dirt, and definitely no more traipsing around the countryside. It's time to get out of here.

Lightning flashed again as she made her way down the ruins and the hill, careful not to slip. Up ahead there was another flash of light, and she saw something sparkle in the weeds. Ashley braced herself on the side of the hill, her back foot pressed into the ground and her other leg bent as she leaned down to brush the withered brown stalks and dirt away. The smell of ozone filled the air. Lightning flashed again. The object looked like gold.

She cringed as dirt lodged under her nails as she pried the object out of the ground.

"Ouch." Ashley dug deep into the ground and came up with a fistful of dirt containing something hard, as a drop of blood welled up on her wrist.

The sneezes came three in a row, and all of a sudden the hair that was tickling her nose, the pieces Mary had so artfully curled around her face, were sticking straight out. A hum ran through her body like the sound of big electrical wires.

The ground rumbled; Ashley sneezed again and lost her balance, rolling down the hill, skirts tangling around her legs as the crazy thought went through her mind that the beautiful dress was going to be ruined. In trying to stop the momentum, her leg hit something sharp, and pain sliced through her thigh.

Cold and wet, she came to as the scene in front of her spun round and round. With a swallow, she closed her eyes and tried again. The ground slowly came to a stop. Swaying, she managed to stay upright until she took the first step, slipped on a stone, and fell again, rolling down the bank toward the sound of water. Something shifted, and the phone went airborne.

"No!" The phone hit what sounded like stone, and then there was a sickening splash, confirming the device's watery death.

Don't panic. It's water resistant, so it's okay.

Flat on her stomach, she scooted forward, blindly patting the ground until she touched water. Pushing up her sleeves, she took a deep breath. The water was icy cold as she felt around, and for the first time since she'd landed in this godforsaken country, something had gone right. The phone had somehow wedged between two rocks. Numb from the icy water, she dried the phone off on her dress and sent up a plea to whoever might be listening.

But the screen was cracked and wouldn't turn on. Her entire life was in that phone. Then she smiled. Everything was backed up to the cloud. She'd find a shop and buy a new phone, and while she was there, she'd find out how to rent a freaking helicopter to get her to the party on time. Were the stores even open this late?

Between the moon winking in and out of the clouds and the lightning, she was able to find her way to the car. Where was the bridge she'd driven over? The stream was there, but no bridge. But bridges didn't move.

Ashley spun in a circle. There was the tree she'd parked under. Except the car was no longer there. Her luggage, laptop, and the purse containing her money and passport. All gone. The night was playing tricks on her. Lightning flashed as she stared at the tree. But no car.

"The damn car's been stolen." All the frustration of the trip poured out of her as she screamed until her throat hurt. Taking a deep breath, she stared at the moon and the shifting clouds until she calmed. The sign must have been a fake to lure unsuspecting tourists to be robbed. Fine. She'd flag someone down and be on her way. When she got another phone, there was a picture of her passport, and she could use the pay function on the phone to buy whatever she needed. Take that, thieves.

But as Ashley sat on a stone wall making plans, something shifted, and the wall gave way as she scrambled to grab on to anything to stop her fall. Pain sliced through her thigh again as a chunk of rock slammed into her. Somehow she grabbed on to a piece of stone and held tight, but with a grating noise it too gave way and the muscles in her throat clenched, nausea rolling through her as a fingernail shredded. The deluge of rain made everything slippery, and it was no use. No matter how she tried, she couldn't hold on. Ashley fell.

Chapter Eight

"Remember the old passage from the cellar that leads to the river?" Christian looked to both his men, who nodded as they rode out of the tavern.

"If anyone asks, tell them 'tis good to have another escape route in case of attack."

There was an old entrance that had not been used as long as he could remember. Christian had heard his grandfather speak of the passage being used for smuggling back in his day.

"Aye, we will see it done." Walter swung up on his horse.

"Make haste to Winterforth. I will follow."

"My lord, you should not travel alone. 'Tis not safe." Ulrich frowned.

"Do as I bid. I will take care." He needed time to be Christian. Not Christian Thornton or Lord Winterforth, but a man. He envied the smuggler, Morien, for his freedom and that he cared not what was said about him. In truth, Christian envied how Morien seemed to be content with who he was, while Christian struggled to live up to his family's expectations and be what his people needed.

He had never spent an entire day lazing about, never had a time in his life when he wasn't a noble, never had a woman see him as a man and nothing else. Did they only care for him because he was rich and noble? The thoughts plagued him as he rode.

On the third day of his travels, he made camp in the wood. 'Twas twilight, his favorite time of day, and he was out walking. When he walked, he found it easier to think on what he ought to do and of all the needs he must meet. As long as he was breathing, none would starve; he would see it done.

He heard the sound of water, and without thought his feet turned toward the sound. The wool would fetch a good price, enough to see the mill rebuilt.

A scream shattered the silence. 'Twas a woman. Christian ran toward the noise to see a woman sink under the water. He kicked off his boots, dropped the sword, and dove in, gasping as the cold stole his breath.

The woman surfaced and went down again, the dress dragging her down to the bottom.

Christian grabbed hold of her and pulled her to him. "Halt. I have you."

Untamed green eyes looked at him as she opened her mouth to speak, but no words came forth. Her teeth were chattering so hard that he thought she might bite through her blue lips. Senseless from the cold, she muttered foolish words he dismissed, until one word in particular made him blink.

Cold much colder than the river flooded through his body. Nay. It could not be. 'Twas not possible.

For Christian would swear he had heard her say the words *phone* and *car*. Unfortunately, he knew both words. His brothers and cousins were married to women who knew well those words.

Yet if she was what he thought, why was she dressed so? As he pulled her onto the bank and rolled her to her side, helpfully patting her on the back, he cursed in every language he knew. He did not have time for a future girl. Did not want the aggravation or the trouble she would cause. For they all caused trouble.

She retched again, mumbling foolishness.

"Apologies, my lady."

Green eyes glared up at him. The color of the forest, deep and full of womanly secrets.

"You're going to crush my bones if you keep pounding me on the back like that."

Abashed, he stopped. "We needs get warm or we will freeze. Can you stand?"

"Of course I can stand. I'm not helpless." She got to her feet, swayed, and fell, crying out. Christian caught her before she hit the ground.

"Mayhap I should aid you, lady." There was pain in her eyes and the way her mouth tightened made him ask. "Are you injured?"

She was cradling her hand to her body.

"When I fell, my nail ripped off, and I cut my leg when I rolled down the damn hill. And I think I also twisted my ankle. I hate the country." Her skin was clear and smooth, the color of a fresh winter snow. Her eyes fluttered closed.

Christian let out a long, weary sigh as he carried her, knowing he was now responsible for her. Let him be wrong and she have a husband or chaperone looking for her. Saints, he prayed she was not a future girl. He was betrothed, and should not note how fetching she looked when she scowled at him.

As he carried her to his makeshift camp, Christian looked for signs of a struggle. Finding none, he sighed, building up the fire to dry them both. The light on her hair reminded him of winter wheat, the locks curling over her shoulder. He looked closer to see pearls woven in the strands. Nay, she must be a lass run away from a husband or set upon by thieves. Her form was pleasing—not that he lingered overlong. And her dress, it marked her as a merchant or minor noble, but he was certain he had heard the words, hadn't he? Or perchance he mistook what she said? When she woke, he would have speech with her and find out.

While he watched her slumber, he made a choice. He would not tell her who he was. He would be Christian, the wool merchant. Not a laughingstock. The names Christian Thornton and Lord Winterforth would not pass his lips. Once they arrived home, he would summon aid. Her sire would come for her...or he would send for his brothers, and their wives would know how to send her back to her own time. He would marry his betrothed and not think on her again.

The girl cried out, and he gathered her in his arms. For a moment the ever-present loneliness within him receded.

Christian cocked his head. There was an odd noise, one he had not heard before, that came from her. The sound was faint. He leaned close and noticed a fine bracelet on her arm. It was the source of the sound. Ear against the bracelet, he heard the ticking sound. It grew fainter and fainter until it stopped. There were numbers on the bracelet with lines pointing to them.

A clock. Unlike any he had ever seen. So small. Why had it stopped moving? The tiny clock loomed large as all of England as the knowledge settled within him.

The fates were laughing at him, for she was from the future.

Ashley woke warm and content, feeling safe and secure. Her eyes fluttered open and she jolted the rest of the way awake. The man holding her wasn't Ben or the model—he was the man who'd saved her from drowning.

The events of last night flashed before her eyes. She remembered rolling down the hill, cutting herself, and then the awful bridge giving way, dumping her into the frigid water. It had been so cold, the frigid waters stealing her breath, squeezing her lungs, and the dress—it was so heavy that it pulled her down even as she frantically tried to keep her head above the water.

The man mumbled in what sounded like French as she eased herself from his arms. He rolled over, and she took a moment to look at him, noticing his face and hair. The blond was almost an exact match to her own color, and just as long. Memories flooded in, and she knew he had blue eyes, full of concern as he told her not to worry, he had her. And in the moment she had utterly believed him, knew she was safe. Why were they in the woods? Was it some kind of primitive campsite? Was he a backpacker or—*please not*—a homeless guy?

Ashley leaned over and sniffed. He didn't smell of body odor, more like smoke and earth and male. Wow, he had long, thick lashes. Why did men always get the perfect lashes when women had to shell out thousands over their lifetime on mascara?

He was dressed in something similar to what she'd seen in Mary's shop. Then she remembered: the theater. But why camp out dressed in costume? So many questions.

"What time is it?" She looked at her watch and blinked back spots, feeling faint as her world tilted. Her watch had stopped at four thirty. It was obviously morning, which meant she'd missed the party and lost out to Mitch.

"My phone."

Frantic, she dug in the pockets of her dress before remembering it falling into the water, the screen cracked and black when she finally fished it out of the water, only to lose it in the fall.

"Hellfire and damnation." She clapped a hand to her mouth. The horrid Southern drawl hadn't passed her lips since she'd spent every penny she could scrape together working a second job during school to pay to erase it years ago. What was happening?

"Don't panic." She'd borrow money from the actor sleeping at her feet, get a phone, and call Mr. Havers. Surely he'd understand an accident. Then she was chartering a helicopter and arriving with a splash. It wasn't too late to salvage her career. For a moment she thought about waking the guy and demanding his phone, but he looked so peaceful that she let him be. After all, he'd saved her life—the least she could do was let him sleep.

Her shoulders slumped and she hunched over, inching toward the fire to dry the parts of her dress that were still damp. Dispassionately, she took stock of the dress, noting parts of it seemed to have shrunk, and the rest was a wrinkled mess, not to mention she'd lost the beautiful belt. But on the plus side, the dirt and mud she had rolled through had come out, so all in all she guessed it all came out pretty even—which was good, considering someone had stolen her car and belongings, so she'd be arriving in what she was wearing. What a story she'd have to tell. *Let's hope the new guy in charge has a sense of humor.*

Careful not to make noise and wake the man, Ashley looked for a path. She wanted to figure out where she was— maybe to the left? But she didn't get very far before the brush and trees were too thick to move through. She turned around and made her way back, knowing she was stuck until he woke. Reaching out, she hesitated. He slept, but it was like a big cat. One second they were asleep, the next pouncing on a mouse. She was in the presence of a wild beast, and when faced with a tiger, she admired the beauty and savagery while fully understanding at any moment the cat could pounce. The man hadn't done anything to make her think he would harm her—in fact, she'd felt safe with him—but this morning, in the light of day, he gave off a different kind of energy, something primal. Uncivilized.

Then it hit her: he *must* be homeless. The guy had been polite, but there was a volatile air about him, like if he was crossed, his enemy would be dead in the dirt without the guy even breaking a sweat. Why was she spending time thinking about someone she didn't even know? She shook her head and sat down. It was cold, she had no clue how to build up the fire, and she heard a rusting in the woods. Scooting close to the man, she decided the unknown monster in the woods was a lot scarier than the sleeping tiger beside her.

When he woke, she could finally leave Wales behind her. Life worked best on a schedule. Feeling better now that she had a plan, Ashley vowed she'd salvage the situation, turn it to her advantage, and show her new boss she deserved the promotion. Mergers. They were hell on earth.

Chapter Nine

Christian woke, tensed, and rolled to his feet, sword at the ready, only to see the woman he had pulled from the water watching him.

He was knight of the realm. He would do his chivalrous duty by taking her to Winterforth, then he would aid her in going home when 'twas safe. *Dolt. You should tell her what you know.*

"Good. You're awake. I need to borrow your phone." She held out her hand, looking most displeased.

Nay, he needs know more about her before he told her what he knew. "Did you sleep well, demoiselle?"

"What language is that you're speaking? You're in England. Are you English?" She peered at him. "Or are you here on holiday?"

He made her a small bow. "Forgive me, demoiselle. Better now?"

She narrowed her eyes, looking concerned she had woken to find herself in a different country, and he resisted the urge to snort. For she had woken to a different time, as difficult 'twas to believe.

"What was that you were speaking first, French? It doesn't sound like any French I've ever heard, and I spent two weeks in Paris last year on business."

He arched a brow. "Would you prefer another language? Mayhap Latin or Greek?"

"Everybody's a comedian. English is fine."

The woman standing before him, with locks of golden hair falling around her shoulders, astonished him. She was like his brothers' wives. Though Anna was not outspoken. A knight would tell her what he knew to be the truth. Ride for the nearest inn and dispatch a messenger. While he did not know how the traveling through another time worked, Christian knew each woman had said there was a moment they could have returned to their own time, but each made a choice to stay. Who knew if this traveling would work the same for her?

If he told her about his brothers, he would have to tell her who he was, and she would hear the jests about him. Robert thought the tales amusing. His brothers did not see him as did the rest of England. A laughingstock. Christian had not been back to court, not wishing to hear the tales or stride by as women tittered behind their hands. And the other courtiers, they would look upon him with disgust, admonishing others to stay away from him, for they now considered him less than a man.

Nay, he would not send for a messenger. Not yet. This

odd girl was the only person he could just be Christian with, instead of Lord Winterforth or one of the Thornton brothers, or the man who was not man enough to make a babe.

"We're wasting time." She held out her hand again. "Did I stutter? I need to borrow your phone."

"My phone?"

"Is there an echo in here? I've got to call my office. They'll be wondering where I am. It's important. Oh, do you have the time?"

"I do not have a phone." Christian looked to the sky. "'Tis morning." He searched through the bags, coming out with food and a flask of water, but after looking at her again, he put the flask back and chose another, one with ale.

"Eat first. You will be hungry, and 'tis a long ride."

"You don't seem to understand. I have to go." She threw her hands up and paced around the small clearing. "I'll grab something on the way. What I wouldn't give for a latte right now. Please tell me there's a shower at this campground?"

He gaped. "Shower?" The sky was clear. "'Tis not raining."

"Not rain. A shower. You know, a bath? To bathe?" She huffed. The look on her face made him want to laugh, but he dared not. She was in a fine temper, and he had no desire to be on the end of a shrewish tongue. From what he had seen, except for sweet Anna, who put up with John, future girls had fearsome tempers.

"You want to bathe? Now?"

"Shower, bath, who the hell cares. I need to shower every morning. It wakes me up, gets me going, especially if I don't have coffee." She glared at him. "You know, start the day off right and not offend your coworkers with your stench."

He discreetly sniffed his person. He did not stink.

"We should go. No stopping until nightfall."

"You have got to be kidding me."

The shrillness of her tone made him flinch.

"At least tell me what time it is so I know how much damage Mitch has done. It's bad enough I missed the party. Maybe I can still salvage this disaster."

The fire out, he cleared away any sign of their presence. Who knew what ruffians might be lurking about.

"As I said, mistress, 'tis morning."

The booted foot she stamped had him wishing to examine the craftsmanship. He wanted to touch the leather, but if he did, she might well kick him.

"Be more specific. You must have a watch even if you don't have a phone. Exactly when in the morning?"

Had his brothers faced such ill treatment when they first met their wives? Were they all so unpleasant at first, these future girls? The men in their time must cover their ears all day long.

"Why does the time matter? We will get where we are going when we arrive."

Her mouth fell open and she shut it with a snap. "Look, you might be homeless or living out some kind of crazy fantasy out here in the woods, I don't know, but normal people care about the time. We have schedules, appointments, things to do."

She stepped forward and poked him in the chest, her head coming to his shoulder. When she had to lean back to frown up at him, he knew it made her angry to do so, from the way her nostrils flared and her cheeks turned red.

"Let me tell you something: the world runs on time. Down to the minute, no, down to the second. Every single day, I have a crazy busy schedule with no room for nonsense."

She seemed to realize she was standing close enough for him to smell her. The scent of roses filled his nose. With a gulp, she took two steps back, breathing heavily.

"We have to hurry. I'm going to lose my job."

"Let us begin with your name and from where you hail." He wanted to see what she would say.

"Oh, right. Sorry, I'm only rude when I'm hungry or really late. I'm Ashley, Ashley Bennett. From New York City." Seeing the look on his face, she rolled her eyes. "You know, in America?"

Aye, he knew this America. 'Twas where his brothers' wives hailed from. Christian looked to the skies, wondering if the bloody fates were laughing at him along with the rest of England.

"Christian. At your service, mistress. What, pray tell, is this important job you must make haste to arrive at a particular time of day?"

While she talked, she sidled up to the horse, eyeing the animal dubiously.

"I'm in finance. My company is merging with a firm based in London, and my job's at stake. It's between me and one other guy, who's a slimy jerk who'll do anything to steal this job out from under me. One wins and the other is out." She snapped her fingers.

While he didn't understand most of what she'd said, he

did understand how important it was to her to go to London. He could aid her. London was four days' ride from Winterforth. Once he took her where she wished to go, then he would tell her how to get back to her own time. Or at least what he knew—it wasn't as if there was a door she could walk through and find herself back home.

"When must you be at this job in London?" He cocked his head. "We are a long ways from there."

As he watched, she sniffed the horse, wrinkled her nose, and stepped back. "I know we're a long ways away. I've been driving around this country forever. It's a long story. There was a storm, so the plane detoured to Wales. Then I got lost and ended up here. Wherever here is."

She seemed to be looking for someone.

"Are you traveling alone?"

"We're not in some backward country. I'm a grown woman, perfectly capable of traveling alone without a big, strong man by my side."

She thought he was strong. He was pleasing to her.

"There must be another person somewhere around here with a phone I can borrow. Point me towards civilization, and seriously, I need to know what time it is."

Christian spoke softly to the horse, packing away his belongings before he turned back to her.

"The monks at the abbey near Winterforth have a water clock that tells time to the quarter hour. Their clock rings seven times a day: matins, prime, terse, sext, none, vespers, and compline, for work and prayers. In London you will find the bells ring for the opening of the markets, at curfew, and holidays."

He watched her as she took a closer look at the bags and his horse, touching the leather. Almost as if she had never seen such things. Robert's wife, Elizabeth, said they had horses in her time but not everyone knew how to ride, instead riding in horseless carriages, which he still did not quite believe.

"Why does the time matter so, mistress? You wake, go about your day, eat, sleep, and wake again. At my home there is a sundial in the garden behind the chapel. I will show you how to use it."

She frowned and shook her head. "I'm still trying to decide if you're homeless, mentally ill, or maybe in some kind of TV show or movie, and I've stumbled onto the set so you're staying in character. Although I have come to the decision you're not going to murder me in the woods."

While she spoke, she did something with her hair, twisting it and putting it up, showing off her face. 'Twas a beautiful face—her eyes sparkled when she was angry, making tiny flecks of gold appear. An uncertain look crossed her face.

"You're not going to murder me, are you?"

"Nay, not this day."

The corner of her mouth twitched. "Good to know. Your home. Is it close?"

"Aye, it will take us a se'nnight if the weather holds. Once we arrive, I will dispatch a messenger for you to contact those awaiting you in London."

"A messenger? Is that code for make a call or send a text?"

"A man on horseback will carry a message."

The sigh escaped as if forced from her body, and he knew exactly how she felt.

"Of course. Why make a call and be efficient when you can send a man on horseback with a piece of paper? Why not send a pigeon or a turtle?" She held up a hand. "Don't answer that. I was talking to myself."

Ashley was still trying to decide if the man who rescued her was some kind of commune-with-nature guy or an actor totally committed to his craft, when he lifted her up on the horse. A ridiculous shriek escaped, making her cheeks burn.

"Have I mentioned I don't like horses?"

He finished tightening the straps. "'Tis a horse or we walk. My carriage is at home."

Carriage? Okay. So Mr. Blue Eyes was definitely an actor, and he was obviously not going to break character. The whole living in the woods with his sword reminded her of an article she read about the guy in *The Lord of the Rings* who did the same thing, probably where this guy got the idea. Only an actor would be so single-minded and infuriating. They were easy enough to recognize—she'd spotted them on the subway or out and about in the city, even dated one or two who'd had small roles in TV shows. And the one thing she knew for sure? They were all the same. Annoying.

Completely self-absorbed.

He swung up on the horse behind her, and as the beast started moving, she slid sideways. A big, warm hand steadied her, the heat searing her skin through the dress.

"Do not fear, demoiselle. I will not let you fall."

The accent was like a cup of hot chocolate, wrapping her up in warmth and totally delicious. The guy might be a self-absorbed actor, but she was totally buying the rough and ready yet super-hot knight character. While an actor might let her fall off the horse, a knight would not. As they rode out of the clearing and through the woods, she looked for any sign of other campers. Not a single tent or faded wood building.

What kind of campground was this? The answer came immediately. Christian wanted to be far away from the other actors, camping rough with only his sword. It would explain the sword and authentic-looking daggers in his boots.

A snort escaped. Did someone from craft services leave food by a rock? In an effort to be discreet, Ashley twisted in the saddle to get a look at his ears. Nope, not pointed, so he wasn't playing an elf.

"Have I seen you in anything?"

"You are seeing me now, Mistress Ashley."

"Funny. I meant, what movies have you done? TV? Commercials?"

"Your speech is odd. I know not movies and TV and commercials. Are they food where you come from?"

"Never mind. I get it, you're staying in character. Fine, I'll play along."

The horse jolted her to and fro as they cleared the woods.

Odd. There were no houses or cars as far as she could see. Not a single paved road, nothing more than a path, and a muddy one at that. No sign of a movie crew. No lights or power lines or cell towers.

Holding her breath, Ashley listened. No sounds of planes, helicopters, or ringing phones. It was unsettling, like waking up to find herself in the middle of an apocalyptic movie. This is why she hated the country. There was nothing to do or see; they were in the middle of nowhere. Had a helicopter dropped this guy off so he could be far away from everyone else? What a diva.

If they were in America, at least there'd be a strip mall or fast food joint by now. But here? A big fat nothing. They passed a man, dressed in similar clothes as Christian, on a rickety cart pulled by a horse.

Okay, she was going with the movie or TV set theory. A theme park would have made the news, even if it was supposed to be a secret until it opened to the public. Christian certainly had the model looks down pat. Oh well, it didn't matter if she was in the middle of a movie shoot as long as they made their way to people. With phones. But no more camping. She despised camping. Her idea of camping was a hotel with no spa services.

The horse shook its head, making her scoot back until she was pressed against her rescuer. As if the animal knew he made her nervous, he twitched an ear and snorted. Animals were unpredictable; give her a subway car any day. She sniffed again, deciding she'd never complain about the smell of a subway station or the back of a cab again as long as she lived.

Smelly or not, she'd ride a horse or a cow as long as the beast got her to the office so she could find out what Mitch had been up to. No doubt he was sabotaging her at this very moment. The guy knew how to network with the old boys' club, she'd give him that much.

Ashley always had a hair elastic around her wrist or in her purse. While she'd been a grouchy snot to Christian, she'd grown tired of the wind blowing her hair in her face. As she reached up to rebraid it, she caught sight of her bangle watch, the one she put on every morning. Would he think she was weird if she buried it and said a few words? It pained her to look at the frozen clock hands; it made her feel like time was on fast forward and she was stuck on slow. Sighing, she coiled the braid into a low chignon.

The wind blew through her, the cold reaching inside of her, turning her organs to popsicles. As if he'd read her mind, he pulled his cloak around them both, the heat flowing into her, as good as any radiator.

The endless countryside combined with the motion of the horse made time stretch and slow. Ashley shifted, her thighs and backside sorer than they'd ever been after an extreme cycling class.

"I swear my butt is numb," she muttered.

He chuckled but didn't answer, which was just as well.

"I don't know how long it takes by horse, but if we rented a car it would only take three hours to get to London, *or four as lost as you were, stupid maps app*—at least, that's what I was told. This horse seems like it's taking an awfully long time. Doesn't he go any faster?"

"We'll get there when we get there. You must learn to take

the day as it comes."

Right. First car she spotted, Ashley was stealing his sword and committing grand theft auto.

Chapter Ten

Christian adjusted his hold on Ashley. An occasional snore escaped her lips as she mumbled something too low for him to make out. First she was cold, then his horse was too slow, and finally she grumbled she would be old and gray before they arrived at whatever rat-infested place he was taking her.

Eventually she fell asleep, sparing his ears from any more abuse. Was this how he sounded when he bellowed at his men? Nay, he could not.

The one thing he had learned about Ashley was not to let her get hungry, for when she was, she turned into a bellowing shrew, and did not find it amusing when he told her such. Instead she retorted that he hummed when he was thinking and she found it most annoying.

The sound of water led him to a small clearing, where he dismounted, lifting her in his arms. He set her on a pile of leaves and covered her with his cloak then took care of his horse.

'Twas late in the day and would be dark soon. Tomorrow there would be an inn, and Ashley could have a bath and a hot meal. He looked to the sky. The smell of snow in the air was faint, and he prayed the weather would hold until they reached the inn tomorrow. They had passed few travelers and seen no one for most of the day, so he went to fetch water and firewood.

The waterfall soothed him as he thought about his guest. 'Twas evident she was unused to sleeping outside. Curious about her time, it had taken all of his considerable control not to ask her questions, for he did not wish to give himself away. He washed quickly, the water chilling him, then brought water back to the clearing.

"Are you hungry?" He spoke softly to wake her. Her eyes fluttered open, and for a moment he wondered what it would be like to see those intelligent green eyes every morn.

"I thought you would like to wash and eat." He helped her stand. "Walk; it will ease the pain."

"I'm starving." She took a few steps and groaned. "You know, I thought I was in good shape, but riding like this, it's like a weekend of boot camp with a drill sergeant from hell." She rubbed her rather fetching backside and rolled her shoulders.

"I'd love to soak in a hot tub for an hour. Or a massage. That would be heaven." A few more steps and she stretched. "I hear water."

Christian pulled her behind him, unsheathing his sword.

"What—"

A bird took to the sky; no other sounds came, so he resheathed his blade.

"Is everything okay?" She looked as skittish as a newborn colt.

"Aye. 'Tis nothing." He searched through the bags and came out with a small wrapped bundle. "Soap. For you to wash. Tomorrow we will reach an inn. Then you will have a bath and a proper meal."

Ashley took the soap, inhaling. "Roses." She threw her arms around him. "Thank you. For the soap and giving me something to look forward to."

He pointed through the trees. "Follow the sounds to the water. I have nothing with which to heat the water. My apologies."

The smile on her face was like the sun coming out in summer, warming him after the long winter.

"I'm just grateful for the soap. I'll make do." She walked through the trees, and a moment later he heard her yelp.

"Oh my gosh, that's cold. You weren't kidding, were you?"

Christian chuckled. "Wash, and I will prepare our meal. There isn't much, though I have plenty to drink. Would you prefer wine, ale, or water?"

"In the middle of the day?" she called out. He heard splashing. "I guess since we're staying in character, I'll take ale. I always did enjoy a good beer."

He had a small fire going. Normally he would not build one when he traveled alone, but she was cold, and unused to being outdoors. So he would risk it.

The smell of roses preceded her. "Sit and warm yourself." He motioned to a log he had pulled close to the fire. Her hair was wet and twisted into a long braid. "Did you go in?" He pointed to her hair.

"I wanted to but it was freezing. So I leaned back and dunked my head under." She handed him the soap and damp cloth. "I used the cloth to wash. I didn't know where you wanted me to put it."

He draped it over a branch to dry by the fire. "You're shivering." He wrapped his cloak around her then selected the choicest morsels.

"You hum a lot."

"Do I?" Christian blinked at her. "So do you."

He handed her the flask. Ashley held it up, touching the leather, then shrugged and took a sniff.

"Bottoms up." She took a deep drink and licked her lips. A drop of ale ran down the corner of her mouth, and Christian reached out with his thumb to wipe it away. She went still and he snatched his hand back.

They ate in silence as if they had eaten many meals together.

Christian was so distracted seeing to her needs he missed the sound until 'twas too late. He caught movement from the corner of his eye and cringed. In all his years he had never been taken unawares. If his brothers found out, he would never hear the end of it. Five men surrounded them. He stared at Ashley, willing her to understand.

"Do not say a word."

She nodded, the bread in her hand forgotten, her eyes huge as she watched the men.

"Give us everything you have and we'll let you live." The leader of the little band brandished a slightly bent sword.

Christian studied every face, marking them men. A blade

poked him in the side. "You heard him. Hand over your gold."

Another man nodded to Ashley. "You too, lass. Give us the odd bracelet. I sees gold on the edges."

She swallowed, but handed them the bracelet and necklace she was wearing. As she leaned forward to hand it to them, something fell out of her pocket, and Christian cringed.

One of the men snatched it, held it up, then scratched his head, his face full of confusion. They all gathered around to look, and he wondered what future trinket she had brought with her.

"What do they have?"

"My lipstick," she whispered.

One of the men touched the red stick. His finger came away red.

"Witch. She is in league with Satan."

This was bad. Christian had heard enough times how careful Charlotte had said they all must be not to change history. And what would happen if someone ever found an object from the future.

"What do you do with the red stick?" he whispered.

"Seriously? This is taking the whole acting thing a bit far, isn't it?" But she sighed and said, "It goes on your lips to make them more red. You know, to make women more attractive to men."

He looked at her lips. They were full and pink and pleasing. Christian shook himself. Nay, he would not think upon her lips. He was betrothed.

The men had their blades out, approaching Ashley.

"Pardon."

The men looked to him.

"I am charged with taking her to the bishop of Winchester. She is a distant cousin and filled with sin."

Ashley gaped at him.

The men peered at her. "Aye, she has an evil look about her."

The men muttered amongst themselves before one shrugged and tossed the small tube into the woods.

"No, I need that."

Christian took her hand in his. "Now 'tis not the time."

She seemed to sense the danger, for she did not argue.

The leader sneered at him. "The sword and the gold."

The sword was Christian's favorite, a gift from his sire, and it pained him to hand it over. But he stood and handed the man the sword, along with the pouch at his waist. 'Twas all the gold he had with him. Why had he not hidden gold in his boot?

"And the dagger in your boot."

Christian handed over the dagger, grateful the man had not seen the other. They examined the goods as Ashley leaned close to him.

"Why did you say I'm full of sin? That's crazy."

He shrugged. "The red color for your lips." His ears burned and he coughed. "'Tis what a woman of low class—a strumpet—uses to darken her lips. I said you were cousin to the bishop so they would not harm you."

"Thank you. But you called me a whore."

"I did not mean what I said."

She scowled at him. "Jerk."

The leader kicked him. "Why so quiet? You fear us?"

Christian scoffed. "Nay, I am marking your faces so when I find you again and take back what is mine, I will slit you from belly to neck and leave you to die in the dirt."

The man snarled, showing a great deal of missing teeth as he took hold of Ashley, who let out a scream loud enough to bring any thief within a day's ride. The men startled, giving Christen the moment he needed. The dagger left his hand, ending the man where he stood. Another was dispatched before the other three turned and ran, stealing his favorite horse.

Disgusted, he wiped the blade clean of blood on his hose. Ashley's mouth opened and closed but no words came forth. She pointed, hand shaking.

"Blood. That's real blood. I can smell the copper smell. There's steam rising from where you stabbed him. They're dead. All dead."

"Not all. Three escaped with my sword, dagger, gold. And my favorite horse."

"Well, I lost my watch and necklace. Not to mention my lipstick." She swayed. "I... There's something very wrong here."

And with that, she swooned.

Ashley came to screaming. The last thing she

remembered was seeing two men fall to the ground bleeding, their eyes open and unseeing.

"Breathe. Slow and easy."

She scrambled away from him, pointing a shaking finger. "Please tell me that was a very realistic stunt with fake blood."

"They would have killed me and done worse to you first. Nay, Ashley. They are dead."

The two man lay on the ground. She nudged the closest man with her boot. When he didn't move, she crawled over, placing her face close to his. It smelled like he'd been rolling around in a dumpster. Taking shallow breaths through her mouth, she placed a finger under his nose.

Nothing.

"He's really dead. I've never seen a dead person before."

All at once, the hundred niggling things that were wrong hit her. She hadn't seen a single light, nor paved road. Not one car or bus, not one normally dressed person. And not a single movie camera or film crew. The scenery seemed the same, but what did she know?

Ever since she'd fallen into the water, Ashley had been cold, but this was different—this was the kind of cold that soaked into her very cells and molecules, freezing her from the inside out. No matter what she did, she couldn't seem to get warm. Was she having an out-of-body experience or hallucinating as she lay on a cold metal table in some sterile hospital?

Christian didn't seem the least bit upset that they'd been attacked and he'd killed two men. As if it were a normal day at the office for him.

She'd heard one of the men tell the others he'd planned to rape her. So while the rational, law-abiding part of her wanted to call for the nearest police officer, another part, a primitive part she didn't even know existed deep within her, was savagely happy Christian kept her safe.

Everything came crashing down, the pieces locking into place with a snap. No matter how unbelievable it sounded, it must be true. Ashley grasped Christian's sleeve, clenching the fabric.

"What year is it?"

"'Tis the Year of our Lord 1334. October. And no, I don't know what time it is. You do not know what year 'tis?"

Why was he so calm?

"Of course I know. Just checking. 1334. Huh. Well, things are starting to make a little bit of sense, I guess."

"Are you going to swoon again, demoiselle?"

She followed him, talking fast, her mouth trying to keep up with her brain.

"I've never fainted before. Not once in my whole life until I met you. Not even when I saw a hockey player get run over by another player. His skate sliced the guy's arm wide open. You've never seen so much blood on the ice."

He'd gone to the pool of water, waded in, and washed the blood from his hose. Christian rinsed off his blade, frowned at her, and pulled her in. The icy water stole her breath, her teeth chattering so hard she couldn't speak. He scooped water, wiping her face, and then she knew—she had blood all over her. From touching the dead man.

"I...I can't."

"Shhh, I've got you." He lifted her from the water and

climbed out. Not knowing what to do or where to go, she stood there staring at him. With a curse, he picked her up and carried her back to the camp, where he built up the fire.

The cloak was gone. The men had taken what remained of their food, drinks, and even the precious little bit of soap as well. Now what? It wasn't like she could flag down a passing motorist for help. Somehow she'd fallen into the water and ended up in Wales, almost seven hundred years before she would be born.

Was this what happened to people who went missing? The ones with their faces posted online? The rational part of her mind knew a percentage of them had been murdered, or were runaways, or disappeared on purpose. The reptilian, ancient part of her shivered, knowing there was a greater power in the world than she had ever suspected. Had others fallen through time? And if they had, what happened to them? Did they end up in the same time as her? Did they go to the future? Or did some of them find themselves in ancient Rome or Greece? Maybe they landed in the middle of the French Revolution? What if a few missing people had gone back even further, all the way to the time of dinosaurs? What must it be like for them? Did they survive? Or die the first day?

Medieval times. Not a good time to be a woman. The fire blazing, she hadn't noticed Christian sitting close to her, watching.

"Why are you acting like nothing's wrong?"

"You suffered a fright and will calm once you are dry. In the morning, we will continue on."

But he acted like someone had taken his last slice of pizza

and then it all made sense.

"It's really not your fault."

He looked despondent. "'Tis my fault. I've never been taken unaware. I have failed in my knightly duties. But do not be distressed. I will find them. 'Twas my favorite horse and my best sword."

While he went on about what he would do to the men when he found them, she needed to come up with a plan. To survive here, Ashley had to accept she was truly in the past. There was a time during the first year after she'd graduated from college that she thought if you took her and dropped her off at her old college dorm, she'd go to her room, speak to her roommate, and head off to class as if no time at all had passed. So while she knew she was addicted to knowing what time it was, she also always had the ability to quickly adapt to her surroundings. To fit in. No matter if it was a boys' club or other place she was unwelcome, she knew how to blend.

When she traveled, she was quiet, taking everything in until she felt comfortable. Immediately going into local shops and purchasing something to wear to look like a local. No ugly American abroad for her. Ashley straightened her shoulders and took a deep breath. She could do this.

"Christian. Where did you say we're going?"

"Winterforth. Four days' ride to London. I will see you where you needs be."

Where she needed to be? Not where. When. Though how did she get back to her own time when she didn't have a clue how she'd traveled through time in the first place?

Ashley wanted to try clicking her heels together or saying abracadabra or some other incantation, but she felt silly, and he would think she was crazy. The last thing she wanted was to end up in an asylum or locked away in a convent. It was a wonder he hadn't thought she was crazy already by the way she'd been acting.

Think, Ashley. From the moment she arrived, she went over everything she'd said and made a note to be much more careful. To listen and learn. Blend until she could figure out a way to go home.

And suddenly Ben, and the merger, her promotion, and even Mitch seemed very far away. Her priorities shifted. All she cared about now was going home. New York was full of jobs. Let Mitch have the promotion. She was smart. Another firm would be lucky to have her.

Chapter Eleven

Christian woke, warm and content, the ever-present loneliness gone. The smell of roses made him smile as Ashley wound his hair around her finger.

"Oh, good morning." Then her eyes went to her hand and she turned pink. "Sorry, habit."

"We should not tarry. It will snow soon."

She looked to the sky, frowning. "How can you tell?"

"Can you not smell the snow in the air?"

"Nope." She sniffed. When she stood, she hopped up and down. "What? It wakes me and helps warm me up."

"Take care of your womanly needs and then we shall depart."

"I'll be fast." Her stomach rumbled but she did not complain, merely walked through the trees to the water.

All morning they walked, and Ashley did not complain once, Christian was proud of her for keeping pace and not bellowing at him. He liked being close to her, hearing her voice.

"You said you did not like to be outside."

She tripped over a limb, and he led her to a flat rock, where he pulled off her boot.

"What are you doing?"

"You are cold. I am warming your toes. Er…"

"Socks." She wiggled her toes. "At…home, I wear a lot of dark colors, so on my feet…where no one sees, I like bright colors."

He had seen such socks before. Lucy had been making them. After running out of people to wear her scarves and hats, she had turned to making socks.

"You asked about being outside. I hate the outdoors, but I live in a large city and am used to walking long distances, though I much prefer to take…a carriage when possible."

Christian thought Ashley might tell him about cars, but thus far she had not told him she was from the future. Mayhap he would try again.

"You said you are from America?"

She fluttered her eyes at him, and he had the feeling she was used to men doing her bidding.

"Did I? No, I meant…another country."

"What country?"

What would she say? And why did he ask? For if she told him, he would be bound to tell her he knew other future girls, which he did not wish to do. Not yet.

"I'm from Greece."

He spoke a few words to her in Greek and saw the confusion upon her face.

"Everyone speaks English in the town where I live."

Nay, he would not ask her anything else. Let her tell him when she would. The longer she waited, the more time he had to spend with her as Christian the merchant.

"I would like to see this town someday. You have done well today." He helped her up and they continued on their journey, the leaves underfoot telling all they were approaching. A while later, they rested by a small stream to quench their thirst.

Late in the day, they passed a small hut. Before she asked, he shook his head.

"Not there. The inn is not far."

She looked at the home as they passed by. "Is that a face carved in the wood?"

He peered at the stump. "Aye, to keep the spirits of the dead away."

"Wait. Is it Halloween? I mean, All Hallows' Eve?"

"'Twas last night. Are you superstitious? Believing in ghosts and spirits?"

She scoffed. "No. I don't believe in ghosts, but in my town, we bake sweets on All Hallows' Eve to celebrate our ancestors."

Two men on horses thundered past them as Christian pulled Ashley close. "Whoresons," he called out, but they were too far away to hear the insult.

They continued onward. The smell reached him before they came upon the inn.

Ashley pulled him forward. "Is that someplace we can stay tonight?"

"Nay, we have no coin to pay for lodging or food." Her

hand was warm in his, and she did not pull away.

"I'm dirty, tired, and hungry. There's something I've been hiding."

Was she going to tell him she was from the future? He would profess surprise. She stopped, removing her hand from his, and he felt the cold wrap around him again.

As he watched, she pulled something from her dress and opened her palm to show him a gold ring.

"I hid it before those men could steal it." She shuddered, and he thought she was remembering the men who had attacked them. "Is it enough to pay for our supper?"

He took the ring, examining the gold band inset with tiny rubies. "Aye, more than enough. With this we can purchase a horse along with a bed and supper."

Christian gave her back the ring. "You should not part with it. 'Tis yours."

"No. It was my mother's, and she would approve". Ashley placed the ring in his palm, curling her hand around his. "I want us to use it."

"I will repay you."

"Don't worry about it. Let's eat. I'm starving."

The heat from so many people crowded in the small inn made him sweat. The smell of meat and ale made his mouth water.

"What is that stink?" Ashley clapped a hand over her mouth. The look on her face made him want to laugh, but he dared not, knowing she was powerfully hungry and likely to stab him with his own dagger if he did so.

"It smells like these people haven't taken a bath in at least a month. And the stale beer. Don't they ever clean the floors?"

"What can I get you two?"

The innkeeper showed them to a small table against the wall, next to the fire.

'Twas like being in hell. Christian showed the ring to the man.

"We were robbed of our belongings except for the ring. We require a horse, a room, and food and drink."

The man held the ring up close to the fire to get a better look. He touched the gold to his tongue and bit down on the ring.

"You were set upon by thieves? There have been many reports the past fortnight." He called to one of the serving wenches, "Bring food and ale. The ring will pay for your needs. The horse has seen better days, but he'll see you where you need to be."

"I'm sorry I wasn't quick enough to hide the rest of my jewelry," Ashley said.

"You did well, mistress." It chafed Christian to allow a woman to pay for his keep. He was a knight. He provided for those in need.

The serving wench brought a pitcher of ale, and Ashley was on her third cup before the food was served.

"You should not drink so much when you have not eaten

since yesterday."

She hiccupped. "I'm thirsty, I'm starving, and the ale cools me off. It's hotter than hell in the summertime in here."

For a moment her speech was different. 'Twas like Charlotte and her sisters.

The food smelled better than it tasted. The bread had small rocks in it but was hot, and the stew was a bit greasy, but it filled his belly.

Ashley wrinkled her nose. "I don't even want to know what kind of meat this is." Before he could tell her, she held up a hand. "No, I really don't want to know." She hiccupped again, humming under her breath. 'Twas a catchy tune that made him tap his foot.

The innkeeper approached, looking downcast and wringing his hands. "A noble has arrived and demanded your room. 'Twas the last one. You will have to sleep in the stables."

"Leave it to me," she whispered, before reaching up to let her hair down, the golden waves tumbling about her shoulders.

Christian couldn't have opened his mouth to protest if he wanted to. Ashley nudged him under the table. The flames cast shadows on her face, changing her, from his Ashley to a courtier who knew how to send men to their knees. She blinked up at the innkeeper.

"Certainly you must have one room hidden away for special guests? What if the king arrived?"

As the man hesitated, hemming and hawing, she reached out and touched the man's sleeve, tilting her head as Christian, the innkeeper, and his wife gaped at her.

"I will sing for your guests. Will that pay for the room?"

"Do you know how to sing?" Christian said.

"Be quiet."

The man's wife snorted. "Are you married, then? Otherwise it would not be fitting for you to be taking this lovely lass to your bed."

"Aye, we're married, nigh on a year," Christian said.

Ashley blinked at him but said naught, for she wanted to sleep in a proper bed this night.

"Well, then." The innkeeper and his wife beamed at her. "Aye, you shall sing and have your room."

"As soon as I finish my meal, I will entertain your guests."

Ashley was thinking, desperately trying to remember lyrics to songs, and Christian kept trying to talk to her. Finally she'd had enough.

"If you don't quit talking to me, I'm going to throw my cup at you. Please, let me think."

"Do you truly not know any songs? We will find another way. You do not need to do this."

She hiccupped again and tilted the cup of ale, draining the cup and setting it down with a bang. It was so hot and crowded. The ceramic cup felt cool against her skin as she pressed it to her cheeks and neck.

"I'm sleeping in a bed tonight. I refuse to sleep outside

again or with the smelly horses." With that, she stood and cleared her throat. "I shall sing for you all."

But no one paid any attention. They were all talking and drinking.

"Take the..." She looked at Christian. "What are these bread things called again?"

"Trenchers."

"Right." Ashley called out to a serving wench passing by, "Take the trenchers away so I may sing, but bring us another pitcher of ale."

"Aye, mistress." The serving wench had the nerve to wink at Christian as she passed by.

Ashley scowled at him. "She better back off." Her hiccups were finally going away. It was so hot in here. She poured another cup of ale and climbed up on the table, planting her feet. Still no one paid her any attention. Fine. She stomped on the wood with all her weight. That got their attention. It looked like a motley assortment of peasants, murders, soldiers, and what she guessed were nobles. And they were all staring at her.

Full of liquid courage, she found a few people in the crowd and met their eyes, putting on her most charming smile. When she was at work, she pretended she was someone else. Not Ashley the studious girl, but her alter ego, Amanda. Amanda was brave and didn't take crap from anyone. She didn't mind Halloween while Ashley hated the holiday with a passion. She spoke her mind, was aggressive and decisive, and didn't let anyone get in her way. Amanda knew how to put Mitch down, and Amanda was going to sing so Ashley could have a hot bath and a warm bed tonight.

Ashley held up her cup, looked down at Christian, and in her voice meant to project to the farthest end of a conference room said, "let's have a song or two shall we, boys?"

There was cheering and whistling as she tapped her foot. All the old-school drinking songs she remembered from dive bars in college ran through her head. Best to start with the song about whiskey. Tapping her foot helped keep the rhythm as the song played in her head. With a deep breath, she opened her mouth and belted out the song.

Halfway through, the crowd really got into it, banging on the tables and stamping their feet. Next she went with the song about the guy in a bar who was on the run. Then the Sally song, and of course a tune by the Dropkick Murphys. That one really got them going, just like she thought it might.

Ashley held out her cup for a refill, but Christian shook his head, turning the pitcher upside down. No, no, no, she needed her liquid courage to get through the rest of this. Catching the serving wench's eye, she picked up the pitcher and waved it around in the air over her head. The woman hurried over, bringing a fresh pitcher, and Ashley went with that song by George Jones about memories.

Unused to singing so much, her throat felt scratchy, and she decided it was time to wind down before the crowd got too out of control. So she sang a song by Hem, then followed it with John Lee Hooker. That had a couple of the men wiping their eyes. For the grand finale, she belted out that song by Thin Lizzy.

The hysterical thing about all this? During her three years of college, Ashley had never spent time in a bar. Always busy studying with her crazy course load, there wasn't time, not with a double major and graduating a year early. Plus, legally she was too young to drink—though she had a fake ID like everyone else, she'd never used hers. But her apartment was across the street from a bar, and she'd had ample opportunity not only to hear the songs they played but to observe people at their worst.

The last notes faded away and she climbed down from the table to shouts and cheers from the crowd. They called for more, but she shook her head, the motion making the room spin.

She bowed and almost fell over, would have if a strong arm hadn't caught her around the waist, pulling her back against a wall. A wall that smelled like winter and leather and horses. She tilted her head back to see cerulean eyes gazing at her, the corner of his mouth pulled up as if by a string.

"You're full of surprises, Ashley Bennett."

His two eyes turned to four. She blinked and shook her head to clear her vision. Totally bad idea. Everything spun, the voices too loud, the heat unbearable. She was way over her limit. All of a sudden all the ale caught up to her. She turned to face Christian, clutching his tunic. "I need air."

The door kept moving. Frustrated, she stumbled, only to be swept up in Christian's arms to the cheers of the crowd.

"Do you always carry women around?"

He grinned. "Only you."

As they passed the innkeeper, he nodded to them. "Fine singing. Such wonderful songs. You shall have your room. My wife is making it ready."

Ashley was too smashed to answer, her eyes heavy. From far, far away she heard Christian thank the man. Once they were outside, the cold night air helped, and she opened her eyes. The revolt started in her stomach and traveled up to her throat.

"Please, put me down. I don't feel so well."

Chapter Twelve

Christian had never heard such songs before. To see Ashley standing on the table before the entire inn, singing, had surprised him, as had the copious amount of ale she consumed.

He put her down, as she bade, but kept a hand on her arm as she swayed in the wind, bleary-eyed and red in the face. Using his sleeve, he wiped the sweat from her brow.

"It's so hot in there. I needed fresh air."

The water from the well was cold. He sniffed; it smelled sweet, so he fetched them a cup.

"Drink. You'll feel better."

Water ran down the side of her mouth as she drained the cup.

"More."

With a grin, he refilled her cup. "As the lady wishes."

Ashley blinked. "I love your accent. You know, you're

incredibly good-looking, like movie-star hot." She swayed again. "You can let go of me now."

The future girl found his visage pleasing. Christian looked down to see more gold in her eyes this night. "Let go? Methinks you would meet the ground, lady."

For a moment he released his hold, and she stumbled. "Perchance I shall keep you close. Thieves might be about."

"You'll take care of them." She fit perfectly to his side, and he had to strain to hear her mumblings.

"I like having you hold me."

In truth, he never wanted to let her go. Ashley Bennett was opinionated, vexing, intelligent, and beautiful. And when she was with him, she banished his loneliness as the sun sent the darkness into hiding. In every way she was his match, and yet...she wanted to go home, and he was betrothed and could not break the engagement without losing his honor. There could be nothing between them, no matter how he wished otherwise.

Ashley had not spoken in so long that Christian thought she had fallen asleep, but then she spoke quietly, almost to herself.

"You know, Christian, I've never cared the least bit about history. Always believed in only looking forward."

"And why is that? History tells us where we have been and warns us to beware going forward."

The wind had blown her hair into her eyes. He took her wrist, pulling the tie loose. It was unlike anything he had ever seen. The cord stretched and, when released, held its original shape. 'Twas difficult to do without letting her go, but he managed to pull her hair back and twist the band around it, as he'd seen her do countless times while they'd traveled together. It wasn't as nice as she made it look, but her hair no longer blew in her face.

"Well you see…" She let loose a heavy sigh, not unlike his king when dealing with troublesome nobles. There was a low stone wall next to the stables, so he lifted her up and sat beside her, keeping his arm around her to hold her close. Only so she would not fall. Truly that was the only reason, he told himself.

"You were saying?"

She stared into the darkness, shivering.

"We should go inside. You are cold."

"No. Just a little longer. It's quiet out here, and I want to talk to you."

The innkeeper had given them a cloak, which Christian wrapped around them both. It carried the faint scent of its previous owner, but it wasn't overly odious, and the night air would carry away the lingering scent.

"Did you know, my mother got pregnant with me when she was a teenager. She was wild, fell in with the wrong crowd and got into drugs. Her family was very wealthy, and they made her go to rehab and give me up for adoption on Halloween. They sent her away so no one would know she was an addict and pregnant, and told all their friends she was studying abroad. It was like I never existed. I never knew her or my real dad. She always refused to name him when her parents asked, and no guy ever came forward. I was adopted by an older couple. They were nice, though I always wanted more. Maybe I'm more like my real mother than I want to admit."

She yawned, and Christian thought about what she had said. To be unwanted and unloved, thrown away, only to find a home with strangers.

"I'm sure your dam loved you in her way. We cannot choose our families; we must find our own way in the world, as you have done."

"I'm all alone, and no matter how many people are around, I'm lonely. I tell myself I like being alone, but... there's something wrong with me. I don't know how to not feel lonely." A tear fell, and she sniffed. "I've never told anyone that before. It's a secret, so don't tell anyone, okay?"

Ashley shook her head and tumbled backward, would have fallen if he had not caught her.

"I know what it is to be alone even when surrounded by those you love. Marriage will help." He prayed 'twould be so. "You have my word. I will not share your secrets."

"You're very easy to talk to. You know when I'm with you, I don't feel lonely. Isn't that funny?"

Before he could answer, she held his hand, looking out into the night.

"I forgave my mother and her family a long time ago, though it still hurts. The couple who adopted me, they were older and couldn't have children. They were very kind, and I loved them. My adoptive father died of a heart attack, and a year later my mother died of cancer. Thank goodness it was fast. I had graduated high school a year early and just started college. She made me promise not to drop out. So I decided to stick with my plan and graduate early. Do great things, and somewhere my real mom's parents would hear about how successful I'd become and wish they hadn't cut me out of their lives so easily."

"I'm sorry. My parents have passed as well. I miss them and do not know what I would do without my brothers."

Thinking she was asleep, he leaned down to scoop her up in his arms when she spoke once more.

"You know, I never put down roots anywhere. I left tiny Pooler, Georgia and went away to school, where I didn't know anyone, and then I took a job in New York City, where I didn't know a soul. It's so exhausting and difficult to form close attachments or make friends. I don't get relationships. Why are they so hard?"

She slid off the wall, gently swaying back and forth.

"So I live for each day and believe everything will work out as long as I work hard enough and have a plan. My five-year plan is my friend."

Ashley crouched down, digging in the dirt.

"What are you doing?"

"It's time for me to quit obsessing about time." She blinked up at him. "I'm having a funeral for my watch. You know, my pretty pink bracelet those men stole?"

"Ah, you should go in, sleep." She was drunk, and Christian did not know if he should pick her up and take her inside or let her do what she needs to. In the end, he decided he would stay with her for as long as she needed. He looked around, found a small spade, and dug the hole for her.

"Thank you. I know I don't have my watch, but I wanted a way to let go."

She patted the ground around her, found a rock, and placed it in the hole.

"Farewell, time. I hope we meet again." She covered the

rock and stumbled when she stood. Christian swept her up in his arms.

"It makes me sad to see time standing still. The hands on my watch were frozen, just like me. But I'm not going to worry about time anymore. I'm going to live in the moment and somehow find a way home."

"'Tis good." He grinned. "You are a strange woman."

"So are you, Christian, but I like you anyway."

Chapter Thirteen

He had her inside the inn and all the way to the steps leading up to the rooms above when she turned.

"I want another beer."

"Don't you think you've had enough this eve?"

"Just one more, then bed."

Christian called to the serving wench, who brought them cups of ale. They leaned against the wall, where he kept one hand on Ashley's arm so she would not slide down the wall.

"I believe you'll regret this in the morning."

"Regrets. The world is full of regrets." She drank half the cup and let out a very unladylike belch. "You know, I don't know why I trust you, but I do. Trusting people has always been difficult for me. But when I do trust, I'm loyal to the end." She poked him in the shoulder. "But if you betray me, I will never forgive you."

She squinted, wrinkling her nose. "I hate camping. I hate

horses. And I hate the way it smells in here. Like old beer, body odor, and wet dog." She leaned into him, so close he could count the three brown spots above her eyebrow. He'd never noticed them before; they were faint and formed a half-circle, calling attention to her eyes.

"I love my creature comforts. Massages, pedicures, spa days. How will I ever get back home?"

"Do not worry. I will find a way to send you back." He took the cup from her. "You have a lovely voice."

"I never sing in public, but I didn't want to sleep outside." She turned a brighter pink. "I'm afraid of things crawling on me while I sleep."

"Aye, the wee beasties can be fearsome."

"You're making fun of me."

"Nay, mistress, I would not jest. Shall we seek our beds?"

She shook her head. He did not let her stumble. All she'd had to drink had softened her edges and prickly temper.

"I hear music. I want to dance."

One of the men was playing a lute, and others were dancing with the serving wenches. Christian made her a low bow.

"Then we shall." He offered her his arm, which she took, and he smiled as she held on rather tightly. The women were in high demand, and before he knew it, Ashley was swept away to dance with others. He leaned against the wall, arms crossed, where he could make sure no one made untoward advances. The amount of ale he had consumed was making Christian drowsy when a slap rang out.

He pushed off from the wall to see Ashley scowling. The man in front of her raised a fist. Christian waded into the crowd, pushing and shoving men aside, as he lunged for the man.

"You will not hit a lady."

"Look who it is. Lord Winterforth, the man who can't please a woman." The man sneered at him. "That's no lady."

Christian's fist met the man's nose with a crack. He pushed Ashley out of the way. "Stay by the wall."

The brawl spread throughout the tavern, hands and fists flying. Christian swore as someone kicked him. Only for a moment did he turn his head to look where he'd sent Ashley out of harm's way, and a fist caught him on the side of the head. Seeing two of the men in front of him, he swung for the middle and caught the man in the jaw. The man in front of him fell, and Christian touched a finger to his teeth; one was loose. He spat blood on the floor and caught the next man, the one who had started this fight, in the face. He grunted and fell.

Cold water hit Christian in the face.

"Bloody hell," he bellowed.

The innkeeper and his wife were dousing everyone with water, breaking up the fighting and bringing the patrons back to their senses.

Blood dripped from a cut above Christian's brow as he made his way to Ashley. She had her eyes shut tight, and as he neared he could hear her humming softly. He stepped over a broken chair.

"Mistress?"

She opened her eyes. "You're bleeding."

"A bit."

She snatched a cloth from a broken table and touched it

to his nose and lip.

"Does it hurt very much?"

"Nay, 'tis naught but a scratch."

The innkeeper stomped over to them. "There will be no room for you tonight. 'Tis going to a paying customer. Sleep in the stables." He cursed and muttered as he kicked a broken bench away.

Christian opened his mouth to say he would pay for the damages, but he remembered that he was not Lord Winterforth, he was a merchant, and a merchant would not have the funds for this. When he returned home, he would send his messenger with gold for the innkeeper.

He swept Ashley up in his arms, to the cheers of the crowd. She couldn't stop laughing as he carried her to the stables.

"What amuses the lady?"

"I've only seen a fight like that in a movie or at a hockey game. It was...so fast." She touched his cheek, the look in her eyes making him cease walking.

"You were amazing. Thank you for defending me." Then she wrinkled her nose. "It smells in here. Like your horse."

He put her down. "The innkeeper threw us out. Welcome to your chamber, my lady."

With a sigh, she flopped down on the hay. "Well, at least it's warm."

He should be able to provide for her, to procure the nicest room, a beautiful cloak, yet he was penniless until they reached Winterforth. Unless he told everyone who he was, but no—he wanted to remain Christian the merchant for a little while longer.

She took hold of his hand, pulling him down next to her.

"I have to tell you something. It's very important."

She looked around to see if anyone was listening. There was a stable boy in the corner, curled up in the hay sleeping. Christian pressed his lips together so he would not laugh as she placed a finger to her lips.

"We must be very quiet. I don't want anyone to hear. They would never believe me."

She looked into his eyes, and he felt his world shift.

"I was on my way to England, for work, when I landed in the water and somehow found myself here." She waved a hand around. "You said it was 1334?"

Christian nodded, afraid to break whatever enchantment she was under. He wanted to hear her story. Why had she waited so long to tell him from whence she came?

"What year do you come from?"

"2016. I don't live in Wales or England. I'm from America, from the greatest city, New York City. There's so much to do. You can find something to eat anytime, day or night. And there are so many people."

She gripped the sleeve of his tunic.

"I love the noise. I love the smell of the concrete, the buildings, and even the terrible subway stations."

Then she nodded at him.

"Oh, right, you wouldn't know what a subway is. It's like a metal box that takes you very quickly from one place to another. And horses?"

She waved a hand, and would have rolled off the hay had he not caught her. It seemed he was always catching hold of her.

"We don't have horses—well, we do, but they're more for looks. Some of the police ride them around the city, and you can take a carriage ride through Central Park. But the general population doesn't use them anymore. We take cars, and cabs, and the subway, and trains, and planes." She widened her eyes. "Oh my goodness. I have to tell you about planes, going to the moon, and books and movies and coffee —beautiful, wonderful coffee."

Ashley pursed her lips. "You're not saying anything."

Had she forgotten she had told him she was from America and then lied and said she was not? Would she remember having speech with him, telling him her secrets, when she woke?

He took her hand in his, surprised at how small it was, the skin soft and unmarked.

"I believe you, Ashley. I am a learned man. There is more to our world than what we can see and touch."

"I'm so glad you believe me. I was worried I would find myself tied to a stake, or you'd try to have me exorcised or put away wherever you put crazy people in your time."

Yet as she talked about her home and why she loved it so, he still did not tell her the truth about himself and what he knew about her.

When she paused, he asked, "Why don't you have a husband?"

She let out a sigh. "I have a boyfriend. His name's Ben. He's a doctor for the Rangers. That's a hockey team." She made a swinging motion with her arms. And went into an explanation he tried to understand, to no avail.

"So that's hockey, and the fight in the inn kind of

reminded me of what happens at a hockey game, sometimes. Anyway." She waved a hand around again. "We're both really busy. He travels with the team and is always working with one of the players, and I work so many hours. Sometimes we only see each other for an hour out of the week. But it's convenient."

This woman from the future had built high walls of stone deep within her heart, guarded by fierce knights. 'Twas only when she drank to excess that she threw open the gates.

"It's convenient, you see. What we have together isn't love. Love is really hard. And relationships are a lot of work. I'm not very good at them. Are you married?"

"Nay, I am not married, though I would like to be. I don't know if marriage is hard. It doesn't seem so for my brothers."

Ashley put her hands on his chest and didn't say anything. The way she was looking at him—it was the way he'd always wanted a woman to see him, the way his brothers and their wives looked at each other, full of love.

"I want to kiss you."

She leaned forward then suddenly sat back, clutching her stomach. And before he knew what had happened, she had thrown up all over his boots.

As she swooned, he caught her, laying her gently down in the hay. Satisfied she was asleep, he went outside to wash. He had not behaved honorably. He wanted to kiss her. Make her his. In the time they had been traveling together, he had come to care for her.

Nay, he was betrothed. He must aid Ashley and send her back to her own time and to Ben. Though the thought of another man kissing her... Nay, she said she did not wish to stay in his time. She would not be happy here with him. So he would let her go.

'Twas not proper to sleep next to her, but she was shivering, so he pulled the cloak over them and held her close, feeling her curves as the smell of ale and the faint scent of roses lingered in her hair. She looked beautiful in the wrinkled, muddied gown with a smudge of dirt on her cheek. He wiped it off with his thumb as she curled up next to him mumbling in her sleep. When she was gone, he would not forget her. He would think of her and wish her happiness, even as the loneness crept back inside his heart.

Ashley woke to the worst hangover she'd had in her life. The sensation of someone watching her made her slowly crack one eye open. Christian leaned against the wall.

"I'm so sorry. I don't normally drink much, and I certainly don't act like a crazy person." She pointed to his nose. "Is it broken?"

"Nay, 'tis nothing. How is your head?"

"Full of stuffing. Did I drink all the ale in the tavern?" She narrowed her eyes. "You look like you feel fine."

"I did not drink as much as you. You had a great deal to say."

What had she told him? It was all a big fat blank.

"I don't really remember what we talked about. Did I say

anything...odd?"

He hesitated only a moment. "Nay, you did not. I can hear you are hungry from here. Shall we break our fast?"

Why had he hesitated? Was he being tactful, or had she told him she was from the future? No, if she had, there was no way he'd be acting like everything was fine. A memory flashed and she cringed. Had she tried to kiss him?

She looked up at him through her lashes. He wasn't acting weird. No way was she ever drinking that much again. Three years of college and she'd never gotten up on a table to sing in front of a crowd. And it ended up being for nothing, because they'd had to sleep in the stables anyway. Wait. The brawl was her fault. That horrible man had made the lewdest suggestion, and she'd slapped him. Then all hell had broken loose.

There'd been one time when she was out with Ben and the team, celebrating a win, and she'd had too much to drink, but this...this was ten times worse. As much as the thought disgusted her, she knew the guys on the team swore by having a small drink with breakfast to get over a hangover.

What she wouldn't give for some Lindsay Stirling playing softly in the background while she popped a few aspirin and slept the day away. Inside the tavern, the debris had been cleared away, leaving two tables and chairs. She cringed. They'd be lucky if they were given a piece of moldy bread after the damaged they'd caused. Stupid guy. Guess it didn't matter what time she was in—jerks were jerks throughout history.

She couldn't hold the smile in—the memory of Christian popping that guy in the nose, defending her honor. Medieval men. She sighed. Too bad she couldn't remember what they'd talked about last night. Oh well, it couldn't have been too important, or he would have said something.

Chapter Fourteen

The innkeeper and his wife were arguing in low voices when Christian found them.

"My apologies for the damage. I have none with me, as we were robbed, but will send gold for your troubles when I arrive home."

The woman whispered to her husband. The man cleared his throat.

"We have had problems with Sir Benton before. He will pay for the damage."

"Might there be some labor I could perform to pay for a meal for my wife and I before we depart this morn?"

The innkeeper's wife threw her rag down on the table, swearing.

"Both our girls ran off during the night, taking most of the food with them. Off chasing boys from the next village." She threw up her hands, "How are we to feed everyone this day? I don't even have porridge."

"Do not worry. I will cook for everyone."

The two of them gaped at him as he strode out of the inn. He had seen chickens near the stables. Since his cook had been stolen away to Dover Castle, Christian had taken turns with his men cooking meals until he found another. They drew straws to see who would do the daily cooking. At first he'd left it to chance, but the food prepared had been inedible at best. He prayed that by the time he arrived, a new cook would be in the kitchens at Winterforth.

"What are you doing?" Ashley touched his arm as he looked behind a barrel in the small courtyard. He wiped the dust on his hose. They both needed a bath, but that would have to wait.

"Seems the cook and serving wench ran away with the food. I informed the innkeeper and his wife we would cook and earn our meal."

"I can't cook. I usually just—" She shook her head and moaned, placing her hands to her head as if it pained her, which it likely did, given the amount of ale she'd consumed last night.

"Never mind. What can I do to help?"

"Come with me. We'll have to make do with what we can gather. Search for eggs while I catch the chickens."

"If you say so." She looked uncertain, but poked at nearby bush. Christian noticed the disarray of her dress, and wished he had gold with him to purchase her a new one. When they were home, he would have whatever she wished made for her. A dress for each day, if she so desired.

While she searched for eggs, he caught several chickens,

and was dispatching the last one when he heard a soft cry.

She was pale, holding the eggs in a basket she had found, a look of despair on her lovely face.

"Do you not have chickens...where you come from?"

"Yes, but they come from the store in a package. We don't have to do that." She pointed to the chickens he had laid at his feet.

"Where do you think the chicken on your plate comes from, mistress?"

"I know where they come from, I just don't like to think about it. Where I come from, you go into the store, give them money, and they give you a nice package with the meat already prepared." She was making motions with her hands as if to show him the size of the package. "I hope you don't expect me to pluck them. I wouldn't have a clue what to do, and I'm afraid I'd never eat chicken again."

"I would not dare offend your delicate sensibilities. There were a few carrots and onions left behind in the larder, and I sent one of the stable boys for milk. We shall have chicken pie this fine morning."

"A man that can cook—now that's impressive." She grinned at him. "Lead on. I can chop vegetables. I can't wait to taste what you're making. Just promise me you'll pluck them outside."

"Aye. The innkeeper's wife can use the feathers."

She swallowed and avoided looking at the fowl. "Whatever you say."

Not once had Ashley complained as she chopped the vegetables and aided him in preparing the pastry for the pie. The innkeeper's wife rolled the dough out and put the pies in the stove to bake. He went outside to wash, yet when he returned he could not find Ashley.

"Have you seen my wife?" he asked the innkeeper.

The man scratched his belly. "Said she was leaving. Perhaps she no longer fancies you and has gone in search of a new husband." The man looked at the door his wife had gone through and clapped Christian on the back. "I'd like a new wife. One that doesn't shout or snore."

Christian ran outside, a hand to his chest to stop the pounding. Would she try to go back on her own? The sound of water made him turn. There, around the corner, he saw her with her skirts hitched up, washing her bare legs. For a moment he could not speak, could do nothing more than gape like a lad seeing his first woman. She was beautifully formed, a goddess come to life. When she pulled her skirts down, he ducked back around the building so she would not know he spied upon her.

Shifting from one foot to another, he counted in his head. Certain he had allowed enough time, he strode into the stables to find her talking to one of the horses, feeding the animal one of his precious carrots.

"You understand, don't you?" she said to the beast.

"What does he understand?"

She whirled around, hand to her face. "You scared me."

"I did not mean to. Apologies."

She turned a fetching shade of pink. With her hair pulled back in what the future women called a horse's tail— No, that wasn't right. A ponytail. It did look rather like a horse's tail as she stood next to the horse they had purchased with her ring.

"I was telling him about my adventures so far."

Would she remember she had told him her secret?

"Your speech and dress are odd. I must ask, mistress—no respectable lady travels alone. Where is your escort? I saw no sign of them when I came upon you."

She turned away quickly, but not before he saw the fear in her eyes. As he watched her, she straightened her dress, brushing at the dirt and stains.

"I ran away from home. My father wanted me to marry a wretched old man I did not love, so I ran."

Christian frowned so he would not grin at the tale she spun.

"Do you not think your sire and dam will be worried for your safety?"

"No, they will be happy to be rid of me. I have five other sisters, and we're very poor. It will be one less mouth to feed."

"Did you steal what you are wearing? For 'tis a fine and costly dress. One fit for a wealthy merchant or minor noble."

"One must do what one must," she said as she lied to him. And yet he did not hold it against her, deciding to let her keep her secrets as he kept his.

"I cannot remember. Did I tell you about my family last

night?"

She took a step toward him. "I'm not sure. It's all a bit hazy, but I don't think so. I'd like to hear about them. I never had— Anyway, I'd like to know more about you."

He held out his arm. "Then come with me, aid me in serving the meal, and while we eat I will tell you tales of my vexing brothers."

When Ashley served the pie to the remaining patrons, Christian watched to make sure none bothered her. The one she had slapped, Sir Benton, had left, along with his men, before dawn. Finished serving, they sat at a small table in the kitchen. He poured her a small cup of ale.

"Just one. I've heard it helps after a night of too much drinking. But then it's water the rest of the day for me."

"Water is good when you drink too much. I learned it well from my brother, Robert."

"How many brothers do you have?"

"There are five of us, like you and your five sisters."

But she did not take the bait, simply smiled, waiting for him to continue.

"Of course, I am the most pleasing. Then there's Henry, Robert, John, and my eldest brother Edward. They're all married, and all but two have children."

What would it be like not to have family? To be alone in the world, as Ashley was? As Christian spoke of his family, he thought she should not go back to New York, where she would be alone. He would find her a cottage, and she could do whatever she wished. Though he felt ill at the thought of her married to another.

Yet as he spoke, he did not tell her about his brothers'

wives, not from whence they came. When they arrived home, he vowed to tell her, but while they traveled, he would remain the merchant.

The way she looked at him made him want to aid her, protect her. But she would return home, marry the dolt Ben, whilst he would marry a girl he had never seen or spoken to. Life would continue, and perchance she would remember him with fondness.

"I wanted to ask you about something you said last night."

She paused, cup in her hand, a wary look on her face. "Did I? What exactly did I say?"

"You said love and relationships are hard. That you must labor over them." Christian shook his head. "I must disagree —my brothers and their wives are in love, all of them married for love. Whilst most nobles marry out of duty or to increase land and title, they all found love, and it does not seem difficult. Yet sometimes they bellow at each other rather loudly."

She shifted on the bench, not meeting his eyes. "Maybe they're just lucky. I think it's only me who finds the whole love thing so difficult." Ashley raised her eyes to him, a shy smile on her face. "But it's funny. It's easy to talk to you."

There was a tear in her sleeve, many stains on her dress, and she was still the loveliest woman he had ever seen.

"Do you ever feel all alone?"

"What?" How did she know his thoughts?

"When you're surrounded by people. Do you ever feel utterly alone? I do. All the time. But with you, I feel whole," she whispered.

Christian did not trust himself to speak. He had dust in his eye, he told himself, as he rubbed his face with a dirty sleeve.

"Aye. I too feel alone. Until I met you."

Chapter Fifteen

The horse Ashley's ring had purchased had flecks of gray in his coat, but he plodded along happy enough from what she could tell. She swore she hadn't thought about what time it was. Not since her singing debut at the inn a couple of days ago. Though she still glanced at her wrist out of habit and touched the now fraying pockets in her dress, imagining the nonexistent phone vibrating with urgent calls, emails, and texts.

Time. Seconds turned to minutes, minutes to hours, and hours to days. Time ebbed and flowed, and there was nothing she could do about it except go along.

Now she accepted the day as it unfolded. They would arrive at Christian's home when they got there. It had snowed last night, not much, just enough to be pretty. The woods were quiet, the occasional bird singing or the crack of a branch the only sign there was anyone else on the planet besides the two of them.

The next thing to figure out was how to get home. It wasn't like she could walk through a doorway and find herself back in present-day Wales.

Mitch, Mr. Havers, and the merger seemed a lifetime ago. Even Ben. By now he'd guessed she stayed in London or broke up with him by disappearing, ghosting. He'd be seeing a supermodel, and she wished him well.

As to the rest of her life? The people she called friends she could count on one hand, the rest acquaintances. Those from the gym and the people she saw out and about. The ones she ran into over and over at the same restaurants and gym classes. There were the virtual friends, made on social media, but she certainly wouldn't call them real friends. What would happen to her stuff if she was stuck here? With no remaining family, she guessed the super in her building would pick through and take what he wanted, then trash the rest. Someone was going to drop to their knees and thank their lucky stars when they moved into her apartment.

Modern conveniences were what she'd miss if she had to make a new life here in medieval England. It was disconcerting to wake up and not have an office or job to go to, not have the constant ringing of her phone. She'd worked through high school and college then started her job in finance three days after she'd graduated—enough time to pack up her stuff and make the trip.

If she could get a message to her own time, she'd tell people to take up horseback riding. It was better than the spa or meditating. Ashley yawned, leaning back against Christian, inhaling the scent of man, horse, and something else that smelled like winter. A scent, she'd come to decide, was the way he smelled. The rhythm of the horse made her drowsy, and she struggled to keep her eyes open.

When she woke, they had stopped, and she found herself on the ground, sitting next to a small stream.

"I didn't want to wake you. The horse needs rest." Christian eyed the animal, and Ashley smiled at the look on his face. It was the same look she was sure was on her face whenever she held up a clearance item in the store—was it worth the price? Would it break right away?

The horse, seemingly unconcerned with being evaluated, went about his horse business.

"I guess I was tired. The riding is getting better." She stood and rubbed her backside. "I swear my legs and my butt have gone numb, and I don't know if I'll ever feel them again."

"Aye, 'tis a rather fetching backside."

A giggle broke free, and she clapped a hand over her mouth, but it was no use. He was so embarrassed at what he'd said that he turned a bright red, and she'd noticed his ears stuck out a little when he was embarrassed.

"Forgive me."

"It's all right. I could say the same about you."

And then he turned even redder.

"I should see to the horse."

Ashley splashed water on her face to help wake her up. It was freezing. Too bad she stank at poetry; she'd like to compose an ode to hot water. Christian had said it was going to snow again. The weather guys on TV would be envious— he seemed to be able to predict the weather just by looking at the skies and smelling the air.

Time had passed and people changed; they could no longer tell the weather from looking at the sky. They moved indoors and to cities, becoming accustomed to modern conveniences. Though if she were being completely honest with herself, she was more used to the countryside than she'd let on.

The secret she kept from everyone was her upbringing and her condition. The teenage mom who died of an overdose, fled rehab, and tried to sell her as a baby on Halloween; being adopted and living in a one-stoplight town. She loved her parents, but they were content to live small, while Ashley had vowed to make it, to live in the biggest city, the only city. Small-town life chafed at her, made her feel like life was passing her by and everyone else was off doing exciting things while she floundered.

Three years and a hell of a lot of hard work later, she'd packed her belongings into a friend's car and swore she'd never end up in Pooler, Georgia again. Vowed never to fail, swore she'd be a big success. And she'd been on the way to achieving all that she wanted, until she landed here. Now it seemed like a lifetime ago. Maybe it was time to build a new life.

She finished washing as best she could, and frowned at the state of her dress. The hem had come undone in places, there were several tears, and the pockets had come out of the seams. Guess the dress wasn't meant for more than standing on stage or attending a party.

Tossing a pebble in the stream, she looked to Christian. He was readying the horse for them to leave. There was one other thing she was keeping from him. A really big deal-breaker thing.

If she could go home, it wouldn't matter, but if she stayed... She knew how much he wanted a big family. And that was the one thing she couldn't give him.

When she was fifteen, she'd had feminine issues and required surgery, the end result being she couldn't have kids. So no matter how charming she found him, it would never work between them, because she wanted to go back to her life and cross off every item on her list of goals, and he wanted a wife and a big family. So she would enjoy his company and she wouldn't fall in love with him. No matter that he was the one guy where being with him didn't seem like work. Talking came easy, and with him she felt whole.

Hellfire and damnation, she was in love with him.

"Mistress Ashley? We should go."

"Coming." With a shake of her head, she stood, brushing off the dirty brown dress. If she kept telling herself she wasn't falling in love with him, it would be true. It was the old fake it till you make it, right?

"Are we there yet?"

Christian smiled, knowing it would not be long until she beseeched him to stop. Over the past se'nnight he had come to know her temper well. Though she no longer wondered what time it was or complained about the horse. There were times she was quiet for a long time and he thought she was thinking of her home.

"It will not be long now until we reach Winterforth."

"Can we stop? I need to use the ladies' room."

He found a safe place where any approaching riders would not see them, and helped her dismount. He had heard the expression before, *the ladies' room*—his brothers' wives said the same.

Her voice came from behind a bush. "Wait a minute. Winterforth? That's the place those soldiers at the inn were gossiping about. You know, that guy they were talking about."

He stiffened.

There was rustling in the bush, and he walked a few paces away to give her privacy. When she returned, he was tending to the horse.

"Come on, you remember Winterforth."

"Of what do you speak?"

"The guy those men were saying couldn't please a woman."

He pressed his lips together. "Nay, they say he cannot get a woman with child. He has pleasured many women."

"Why are you getting so defensive? It's not like you know the guy."

But something on his face must've given him away, for she pursed her lips.

"Oh, you do know him."

Instead of answering, he stomped about.

"Is he your boss?"

At his blank look, she tried again.

"Your lord?"

"Nay."

"Oh my gosh, don't tell me it's one of your brothers?"

"Nay, none of them. I no longer wish to speak on the matter." He lifted her back on the horse and climbed up behind her.

As they rode, she kept asking questions to vex him.

"Who cares if this guy can't have kids? Why does it matter?"

He snarled in her ear. "Why? A man is not a man if he cannot get a woman with child, just as a woman is no woman if she cannot bear babes. 'Tis our duty to have children, to carry on our name."

When she spoke, her voice was so quiet he had to lean close to hear her words.

"I didn't know you felt so strongly."

"How could you? You are a stranger to my land."

He felt her stiffen, but she did not say anything, choosing to keep the secret from whence she came, the one she'd told him when she was in her cups.

And she did as he had seen Robert's wife Elizabeth do many times: she changed the course of their speech.

"So where is Winterforth? Is it close to London?"

"Four days' ride from London. It controls a vast expanse of land. You will see its bridge controls the only way across the river."

Chapter Sixteen

Ashley had come to recognize the tone in Christian's voice when he was angry. Spending twenty-four hours a day with him, she'd learned his moods, knew him better than Ben. By the tic in his jaw, he was not just annoyed, he was furious. Who owned Winterforth and why were they so important?

It hurt deeper than she thought hearing him say a woman wasn't a woman if she couldn't have kids. Her heart sank knowing how important children were to him. Deal-breaker territory. For her, a deal breaker was a guy who wasn't ambitious or didn't want to work. With those lines drawn, there could be no future for them, since she could not give him the one thing he wanted above all else. Not being able to have children had never bothered her before...not until today.

While other little girls played pretend weddings with dolls and dreamed of getting married and having families,

Ashley used to play school and office. An old, battered briefcase belonging to her dad went everywhere with her. When she played, she was always the teacher or CEO of the company. There wasn't a single instance she could remember she'd ever played wedding or even thought about getting married.

Sure, she'd thought someday she'd get married. And later, when she knew she was unable to have children, she accepted her new reality and went on with her life. There was a woman at work who couldn't have children and desperately wanted them, and it was heartbreaking. Ashley wished the woman could have her heart's desire.

But her? She'd never felt the yearning for a child of her own. To hold flesh and blood in her arms, knowing she and her husband had created the baby. More power to all those who wanted to procreate, but not her. Two of her friends from college got married when they graduated and immediately got pregnant. When she held their babies, Ashley thought they were cute, but that was it. All she thought about was how much sleep she would lose and how much time she would have to devote to another human being.

Happy being childless, Ashley respected others' wishes to have babies. Saw the joy it brought her friends as they went on and on about how having a baby had changed them. Made them less selfish and more aware of the world around them. No longer self-absorbed. While she hoped she had grown out of that phase over the past couple of years, Ashley didn't know if having a child would change her—or would it? But in the end, it didn't really matter, because she would never know. Being with Christian made her wonder if she hadn't had surgery so long ago, might she have made different choices or felt differently?

Maybe some people just weren't meant to have children. She'd seen a few parents she thought would've been better off never having kids, and she'd seen others that didn't have kids that she thought would be wonderful parents. Tired of thinking about it, she was about to ask Christian a question, when they rode through the trees and there was a massive fortress.

"That's a castle."

"Aye, 'tis Winterforth."

"You didn't tell me we were going to a castle."

Before she knew it, they came to a bridge over a river. She looked down, remembering the last time she'd been on a bridge over a river. It hadn't ended well. They rode across, and she clenched her hands together as the horse's hooves clattered on the wood, and over and over she repeated the same words: "Please don't let us go over."

The bridge held, and they passed under a pointed gate and into the castle proper. There were people everywhere, running around doing who knew what. The clang of metal was loud as a group of men fought with swords. A few were shooting arrows at targets, others wrestled, but her attention was pulled back to the men fighting with swords.

Her breath came in shallow gasps, the scene in the woods clear in her mind, the one that ended with two men dead.

"Breathe. You are safe, Mistress Ashley. I will not let you fall."

Christian. He knew she was about to hyperventilate. A

few deep breaths and Ashley's mind processed the scene. A living, breathing, functioning castle. While she'd never been one for history, sitting on a horse with a medieval man in the middle of a castle courtyard certainly gave her pause.

Up until now she had accepted she was in the past, tried to blend in. But there was something about seeing a functioning castle that made everything seem permanent. Christian lived in an actual castle. On a day-to-day basis.

Something else bothered her as they rode into the courtyard. Something wasn't quite right. Ashley couldn't put her finger on it, was trying to figure out what it was, when a man approached.

"My lord, I sent men out to search for you when your horse arrived riderless."

"We ran into a spot of mischief, nothing to worry over." Christian grinned. "Mayhap next time the thieves will think before they steal from a Thornton."

Ashley was a tornado forming in the sky ready to touch down and obliterate everything in her path. Oblivious to her mood, Christian dismounted and lifted her off the horse, and it took everything she had not to kick him in the gut.

While she stood there fuming, another man approached, a small man with what looked like scrolls of paper in his arms. He made a little bow in front of Christian.

"My lord, I am pleased you have returned unharmed. A messenger arrived a few days ago to bring wondrous news. Your betrothed will be here in a se'nnight."

"We must be prepared." He looked at Ashley and frowned. "Mistress Ashley requires a dress. See it is done."

"Of course, my lord."

She'd had enough. "My lord? Betrothed?" Ashley glared and poked him in the chest. "Who in the hell are you? Did it slip your mind to tell me these little tidbits?"

The little man looked at her with a sniff. She didn't know how he did it, since he was a good six inches shorter than she, but he looked down his nose at her and sneered.

"You, lady, have been traveling with Christian Thornton, Lord Winterforth." The man turned his attention back to Christian. "Shall I have a bath prepared?"

She stamped her foot, and it felt good. Really good. Now she knew why he stomped about and bellowed all the time. Ashley poked Christian again.

"You lied to me, you big jerk. You've been lying to me since we met." She clapped a hand over her mouth. "To think I thought about staying with you. How could I be so stupid."

"Later," Christian said to the man.

Then he took her by the arm. "'Tis not the place. Come with me."

She didn't have much choice, since he practically dragged her into the castle. They entered a huge room—the great hall, maybe? And not for the first time since arriving in the past, Ashley wished she'd taken more of an interest in history. Wished she'd paid more attention to the dates and the events of this time.

The inside of the castle wasn't at all what she expected. She had thought there would be dirty floors, snarling dogs, and gray stone, dripping water everywhere. But it wasn't at all like that. The room they passed through would have made her happy to curl up in front of the fire with a good book, though it was chilly, even with the fires roaring.

The floors were stone, the walls were painted and paneled in wood, and there were tapestries and paintings hanging on the walls. There were multiple fireplaces with fires crackling, large enough she could have fit a whole group of supermodels and a sports car in one of them. People nodded to him, welcoming him back as they openly stared at her, the curiosity plain on their faces.

Ignoring them all, Christian dragged her through the room and up the stairs, where they came to a door. He shoved it open to show her a bedroom.

"Your chamber while you are at Winterforth."

Ashley stepped into the beautiful room. There was a large, heavy bed, a small trunk at the foot of the bed, and a table with a pitcher and basin. She pushed down on the bed.

"I was expecting straw, but it looks like you have a real mattress and bedding. I'm going to sleep like the dead tonight." She whirled around. "But I'm still angry with you."

"Hrumph. 'Tis not as extravagant as the king, but 'twill do. There is straw on the bottom with a feather mattress on top. You will find the sheets linen, the pillows made from feathers." His mouth twitched—he was likely thinking of the chickens, but was wise enough not to laugh. "And woolen blankets to keep you warm."

She looked around, noticing a pipe coming out of the wall, but didn't see any entrances to other doors.

"Where's the bathroom?"

He led her down the hallway and opened another door. It didn't smell as she thought it might. The rush of cold air coming through the window open to the outside was probably why. The fresh air carried away the stink.

"The garderobe." He pointed to a stone bench with a seat in the middle. "'Tis covered in cloth; the waste falls down the chute into a barrel, which is emptied into a pit. There is plenty of wool and linen to...wipe, along with the jug of water to wash when you are done."

His cheeks were pink, his ears stuck out, and while it used to be cute, now he looked like an elephant—at least, that was what she told herself.

At the end of the hallway, he opened another door. Immediately, she knew the room was where he spent a great deal of time. It had that faint scent that reminded her of him, and it was the most masculine room she'd ever seen—and that was saying something, given Ben's man cave.

"My solar." He led her to a chair in front of the fire, and she frowned. She looked at the cushions on the chair. They reminded her of chairs she'd seen in stores back home, which was completely crazy.

"I beseech you, sit and listen."

While she sat, he paced back and forth in front of the fire, his boots not making a sound on the priceless-looking rug.

Christian ran a hand through his hair, making it stick out. He sighed.

"I simply wanted to be Christian. Not the laughingstock of all of England and Wales, and probably Scotland and France by now as well."

"You should've told me. You lied to me."

"Aye, I did. Yet I would ask, is there anything you wish to tell me?"

She blinked at him, startled. "Me? No. Why?"

Christian stomped over to the door and flung it open,

bellowing into the hallway for wine. She was about to tell him he needed to go find someone instead of yelling, when a few minutes later a servant hurried in, breathless, carrying a tray with two goblets. It was good to be the lord of your own castle.

They sat in silence, the only sound coming from him tapping his fingers on the wood chair. Finally, as if he had decided something, he leaned forward, hands on his knees.

"The night you were in your cups. You told me from whence you hail."

Her hand jerked, and the wine sloshed onto her sleeve and into her lap. But the dress couldn't get much filthier at this point, so she blotted it and ignored the stain, which kind of looked like she'd been stabbed. Nope, not going there.

"I did?" She was afraid of what he was going to say, yet somehow she knew.

"New York City. The Year of our Lord 2016."

She grasped her knees to her chest, curling up into a ball in the chair.

"I can't believe I told you. I've been trying so hard to fit in. I'm afraid to ask—what else did I tell you?"

He told her the rest, about her upbringing, but not about the other thing. Relief poured through her body even as the sharp look on his face told her he suspected there were other things she wasn't telling him. And there were, but they weren't things that were really important. At least not anymore. Because he had a damned fiancée. Ashley did what she always did when she felt threatened: she went on the attack.

"Quit making this all about me. What about you? Did it

somehow slip your mind you have a fiancée?" she thundered, her face hot and palms sweaty.

"Let me make plain—"

She stood, gripping the silver goblet so hard she was surprised she didn't dent the thing.

"I can't do this right now. I need air."

Christian bellowed, and this time a teenage boy appeared.

"Don't let her out of your sight."

"She's powerful angry." The boy grinned. "Women."

Christian scrubbed a hand over his face. "Aye, women."

She whirled around, stomping and grumbling down the stairs, through the hall and outside as the boy ran to catch up with her. He held the door for her as she stormed out. They walked around the castle grounds, but she felt trapped and closed in.

"Is there someplace we can go to get higher? To see more?"

She knew what it was like to be laughed at. Had put up with it at her job, which was dominated by men. And if she really thought about it, she was mostly angry because she knew she had fallen for him. Begun thinking about what it might be like to stay, give up everything she cared about. That was, until she found out he was engaged.

Up on the battlements, the boy gave her his cloak. "To keep you warm." He frowned at her. "Might the lady want to change clothes and have a bath?"

"Thanks for the cloak. Do I stink?"

"A bit."

"I know. First I need to think, then a bath, a gown, and food."

He leaned against the wall, crossing his arms over his chest. He looked so much like Christian that she had to bite her cheek to keep from laughing. The boy obviously had a severe case of hero worship.

"I will be here while you pace, lady. Even if we are here all night."

Chapter Seventeen

Ashley didn't know how long she'd been up here, only that she could no longer feel her toes and it was dark. Hungry or not, she wasn't ready to face him.

"I brought warm spiced wine." Christian held the cup out to her.

Talk about the devil himself. The wine warmed her and took away the anger. Why be mad at someone she had no chance of a future with? Maybe they could be friends and she'd attend the wedding? Not. She planned to go home before then. Somehow.

"I wanted to tell you, but I was afraid you would think I was a witch."

"You don't remember, so I will say so again. I am a learned man and I have seen things which cannot be explained, so yes, I believe you."

She'd been thinking. "Which Edward is king?"

"Edward III."

"It's sad. Castles will fall out of favor as cannons come into standard use. There is so much uncertainty ahead."

He looked around to make sure they weren't overheard. "What else do you know of my time?"

"Only the highlights, I'm afraid." She sat on the wall, looking out into the darkness, unable to believe all of this was his. "I never paid much attention to history in school. I'm a big believer in looking forward, not back. If I'd been born in Europe I would know more, but as an American, I don't know why, but we tend to pay less attention to history, even our own. I don't know if it's because we're a younger country or because the country is large. I don't know."

She readjusted her hair, taking out the elastic and quickly doing a messy bun so it would quit blowing in her face.

"I know there's war coming. And the plague. I know this is your life, but to me it was a story in a book, and not a particularly interesting one at that. I was always more interested in meeting the next item on my list of goals."

"Are all women in your time educated?"

"Many. I finished high school a year early—college too. I'm twenty-three."

She looked at him, realizing she didn't know how old he was.

"How old are you?"

"A score and four."

The light from the torches cast half his face in shadow. It was hard to tell how he was taking all this information.

"So you do not have five sisters and are running away from marriage to an old man?"

"No, I made it up to blend in."

She'd fallen in love with him. A guy who was getting married. Well, she wasn't sticking around to see the perfect, beautiful, intelligent fiancée arrive. And to make it all worse, she'd probably be nice on top of it all. Because Ashley couldn't imagine him marrying someone who wasn't all those things. It was time to go home, give up the daydream of living in the past, and go back to real life. How? She didn't have a clue.

"Christian, I want to go home."

"And if you cannot?" His voice was soft.

"Then I will have to find a job. Something useful."

He touched her cheek, and she saw the wetness in the torchlight. Ashley hadn't even noticed she was crying. He stood so close that she could see the gray flecks in his blue eyes, his expression inscrutable.

"I will send word to my brothers. We will return you to your time."

"But what can they do? It's not like they have a time machine."

Christian sighed. "We will talk more after supper."

He dismissed her guard and led her back to her room, where he stopped outside the door. It was strange knowing she would be sleeping alone for the first time since she'd arrived.

"I've had a bath prepared."

Without thinking, Ashley hugged him tight.

"I could almost forgive you for not telling me about your soon-to-be wife." She rubbed her hands together. "It's like Christmas is coming early. A bath. Thank you so much."

He looked stunned, but nodded. "The women will aid you." He turned on his heel and left the corridor, and for the first time she was alone, and the emptiness he left in his wake was enough to fill a stadium.

"We will bathe you, lady."

The two girls looked young, Ashley guessed early teens. They helped her undress. One held up the dress, frowning. "I'll take this to be cleaned."

The other one handed her another round ball of rose-scented soap. Ashley wanted to kiss the girl.

"Shall I wash your hair for you?"

"Please." Having someone else wash her hair was a decadent feeling. As she soaked in the tub, watching the water turn gray, Ashley felt her muscles relax, the heat doing its job.

While the girl scrubbed her—which was a new experience, as she'd never had anyone bathe her before— Ashley thought about going home, started making lists in her head. Christian. It would have never worked anyway, since she couldn't have babies. He'd made it clear he wanted a big family.

The water was cool by the time she climbed out, her fingers wrinkled. The girl dried her off with a large piece of cloth.

The other one had brought something for her to wear. As they dressed her, one of the girls made a clucking noise. "The dress is too short, lady."

Ashley looked down to see her ankles showing.

"It doesn't matter. It's clean and it fits. I thank you for the dress."

"When the merchant comes, you may choose the material for new dresses."

"That would be nice." She planned to be long gone by then.

One of the girls combed her hair, braiding it and pinning it up, chattering away, the sounds washing over Ashley.

"Did you know there's to be a wedding, lady?"

The other one chimed in: "Lord Winterforth is finally getting married."

Ashley snorted. "Tell me something I don't know."

The same guard who escorted Ashley around the castle was waiting outside her door, leaning against the wall, when she emerged from the room.

"The dress is lovely, though you're rather tall for a woman."

Ashley looked down at her stocking-covered ankles. She'd let the girls take her boots to be cleaned, so she was wearing soft shoes that reminded her of slippers.

"I'm not tall where I come from." She was five seven, and in New York she often felt short when she ran into a model on the street. It was an easy breed to spot, the girls impossibly thin and incredibly tall. During her time here she'd seen plenty of people of average height and just as many short ones, though Christian and some of his guards were over six feet. She guessed there would always be outliers.

"I don't know your name. I'm Ashley."

"My name is Quinn, lady. We are to sit at the high table with my lord."

He led her through the great hall as she stared at the transformation that had taken place while she was bathing. Tables and benches that had been pushed up against the walls earlier were now in rows, running up and down the hall. Many of the people she had seen since she'd arrived were already seated. There were tablecloths on the table, and from the dishes and the amount of food being served, she figured out Christian had plenty of money. Not that the castle didn't give it away, but he could have been one of those titled but poor guys. He didn't act like some of the guys she'd met at home that flaunted their wealth. The hedge fund guys were the worst.

Ben's face flashed in front of her eyes. He was going to be surprised when she finally made it back home. Though as practical as he was, by now he'd probably moved on to someone else. Ashley waited a moment to see if she was upset, but she wasn't. That alone told her she had been coasting through life with him. She heard Christian laughing with a couple of his men as they approached the table. Yep, she was upset thinking of him married to someone else. Sad to leave him.

The table at the front of the hall was fancier, with a linen tablecloth, silver goblets, and actual plates. The other tables had trenchers. At the end of the meal, Quinn said, they were given to the poor in the villages and the animals.

Christian stood, as did the other men. He pulled out the chair next to him.

"You are beautiful."

"Thank you. It feels good to be clean again."

Ashley couldn't have said what she ate. She was too busy looking at everyone, taking it all in. The memories would sustain her when she went home. First thing on her list? Diving into history.

Christian and everyone in the castle would be long dead when she went home. Would there be any mention of Winterforth in a book? Did she want to know Christian and his perfect wife had three adorable kids and lived happily ever after?

"Is aught amiss?" The look of concern on his face made her want to run from the hall.

"No, I was just thinking."

"Of your home?"

"And other things." She sipped the wine. "Tell me about growing up here."

His face brightened. "My sire owned several estates, and this was one of them. When I came of age, 'twas mine. Each of my brothers has a castle as well."

She grinned. "Of course they do. I vaguely remember you telling me you had brothers, but not much else, too much to drink that night. Do your parents live close by?"

"Nay, they passed years ago."

"I'm sorry. I know what it's like to lose those you care for."

He was interrupted by a man asking him a question, and

Ashley turned her attention to the people, watching them and learning so she would fit in while she was here. For however long that was. Christian was deep in conversation with the man next to him. She touched him on the shoulder as she got up.

"I'm going up to the battlements for some air."

"Don't stay long, you'll be cold."

Quinn followed, still chewing.

"I'm going up to the battlements. You don't need to follow me."

"I am to guard you—where you go, I go."

"Let's go to the kitchens first so you can finish your meal."

He snatched up the trencher from the table, and she followed him into a bustling room. It was warm in the kitchen, and fascinating watching what everyone was doing. Everyone had a task, and she wondered if they were born to it. She made a note to ask when she had a chance to speak with one or two of them alone. She didn't want everyone gossiping about the weird girl.

Ashley finished her wine while Quinn finished his meal. When he was done, he led her up to the battlements and took up his customary place against the wall.

At the far end of the wall was another guard. The moon was out tonight, and she'd never seen so many stars. Content to just be, Ashley figured it would only take days after she returned home until she was back to her obsessive self, always needing to know what time it was and frantically crossing items off her list. What else would she do? Move upstate and start a farm? No, she'd meet her goals and forget the past...and a man with blue eyes who had touched her soul.

Quinn was talking to another man—they had their backs turned away from her and the other guard wasn't paying attention, so it was now or never.

Ashley looked at the moon, closed her eyes, and made a wish. For good measure, she tapped her heels together three times, hoping maybe the person who had written one of her favorite books had been a time traveler like herself.

But when she opened her eyes she was still standing on the battlements, and there were still men with swords. What was she going to say to the authorities when she made it back? Would she show up the same day and time she'd left? Or would the days missing be the same? If she returned at the same time, she'd simply go on her way to the party and beat Mitch out of the promotion. But if it was later...she better come up with a story to tell. Because there was no way she was telling everyone she'd landed in medieval England, not unless she wanted to find herself locked up for evaluation.

On that thought... Were all the mentally ill people really ill? Or were some of them time travelers who'd made the mistake of telling what they'd experienced?

While she walked back and forth, she thought back to how she'd found herself here. There was nothing that stood out in her mind other than the storm. She'd been digging up something golden. Ashley rubbed her thigh, the cut now a scar. Then again, what did she expect—flashing lights with a sign saying *Time travelers enter here*?

So if there wasn't anything that stood out, wouldn't it

reason that she could easily go back? Was it a matter of will? Ashley knew she was stubborn, to her detriment at times. She had to do things herself, couldn't take the word of others.

And so she sat on the wall pressing her hands against the stone, and thought of home. Summoned up the inside of her apartment. The food truck that sold lobster rolls on the corner, the aroma of melted butter so strong she swore she could smell it, and the sounds of the city. The honking, yelling, all the different cultures together in one place. She could see it clearly in her mind.

"I want to go home. I'm back home where I belong."

She opened her eyes and slumped on the wall. She was still here.

"I could've told you that wouldn't work," Christian said.

"Well, I had to try, didn't I?"

He sat down beside her. "My brothers may know the way for you to go home."

"You said that before, but how could they?"

"You can ask them." He fidgeted and wouldn't meet her eyes. "Do you know I've never seen my betrothed?"

"How can you marry someone you've never seen?"

"James and Melinda arranged the match." He turned to face her. "I have been betrothed five times. This is the sixth. They all run away."

"Why?" Then she remembered. "Oh, because of what's being said about you? But I thought it wasn't true?"

"It isn't."

And he went on to tell her the story.

"And so that is why every lass in the realm will not wed

me."

"Well, that's just ridiculous. And I agree with your brother Edward. You should've gotten someone pregnant then married her."

"That is what they all said. But I told you why I would not." He fiddled with the hilt of his sword. She noticed he had another very similar to the one that was stolen.

When he spoke his voice was low, and she smelled the wine he had with dinner and the scent of spices from the meal on him.

"I wished you to know I do not love her. I hope she and I will like each other in time. Marriage is the natural progression of life. We marry and have babes, continue our name. 'Tis a duty. My brothers wed for love, but I have not been so fortunate. My only hope is that my wife and I will care for each other in time."

"You said your brothers married for love. Don't you want to as well?"

"Of course. But none will have me. And in truth, love is not necessary for marriage."

"You know, it's funny—I used to think the same thing about relationships. But it must be something about this place, because I've changed my mind."

"'Tis late. I will see you to your chamber." As they passed Quinn, Christian paused. "Seek your bed and guard the lady in the morn."

At the door to her chamber, he opened his mouth then closed it.

"I wish..."

"Don't. Wishing doesn't change anything."

He nodded and turned to go.

"I never had regrets until I met you," she whispered as she closed the door behind her.

It wasn't until she was in bed that she realized she'd never gotten an answer. She pulled the covers up under her chin and thought about it. Why hadn't Christian explained why he thought his brothers could help her? Had they met someone else like her? She planned to find out tomorrow. Because there was no way she was sticking around while the guy she was in love with married someone else. Until she could get home, she would hide her feelings and pretend they were friends.

Was she really in love? She never had been, so maybe this was just a remnant of him saving her. She'd heard about women falling for cops or firefighters who rescued them. This was the same.

Wasn't it?

Chapter Eighteen

"Walter, did you see to it Mistress Ashley is in her chamber?"

His guard nodded. "She is, my lord and I sent Quinn to seek his bed." With torches lit, they made their way down the stairs through the hidden room of the cellar to the old passageway that led to the river.

"The passageway has been cleared. All is prepared."

Ulrich turned and nodded. The torches cast light on the damp stone. The sound of water running down the walls, and the sense of someone watching him, made Christian uneasy. His guard looked tense, and then Morien stepped forward, the man moving without making a sound. It was unnerving.

"Thornton."

Christian nodded. "Are we ready?"

The smuggler inclined his head, and his men filled the passageway. Walter led them deep into the cellar to the hidden room where they had stored the wool Christian had held back from selling this summer, in anticipation of such a venture.

The smuggler crossed his arms across his chest, his face half hidden in shadow as he eyed his men scurrying to and fro.

"What would ye have done if we had not met?" Morien pointed to a bundle of wool as it passed through the passageway and was loaded onto the barge.

"I would've sold it next summer at Westminster, as I have always done."

Ulrich returned, his steps echoing in the passageway.

"I have had a word with the rest of the guards. They believe you will not be able to keep this secret from the rest here at Winterforth for long. A few have been asking questions."

"Soon enough, we will swear all of Winterforth to secrecy. They will understand what is at risk."

The smuggler's men were quick, and the wool was loaded onto the barge. Christian stayed, watching as they pushed away, making no sound. He turned to his men.

"'Twas a good night. The gold from this partnership will see Winterforth and its inhabitants through the winter and spring."

Christian had one last task to complete before sleep would be his. A widow in the village did not have money to bury her husband, nor food to feed her children. He dressed in a pair of old hose and tunic, clasped a black cloak around his shoulders, and rode out on the black horse.

The stable boys were used to him riding out at night, as were his guards; the men at the gate greeted him with a soft "my lord," raising the gate only enough for him to pass under. His hood up, he rode for the village, turning back, searching for one window. 'Twas dark, Ashley was asleep.

He had heard what she did not mean him to. Regret. Aye, he understood it well, for he felt the same. What could he do? Not call off the betrothal; it would impugn his cousin's honor and his own. Nay, he must keep to his commitment and marry the girl, though he wished for the first time that the girl would run, as the others had before her, leaving him free to woo and marry Ashley.

The village was quiet, all asleep, as he rode through the streets. While he knew one of his guards could have seen to the task, Christian needed to do this himself. 'Twas his responsibility to care for all those not only at Winterforth, but in the villages as well.

The home where the widow lived was dark, and no smoke rose from inside, so likely she could not afford to keep a fire going day and night. The horse tied to the post, he lifted the latch on the door, placing the bundle inside on the floor. In the morn, she would find food and enough gold, enough to pay not only for the funeral but to feed her children. Enough until he found her a place in a household doing laundry or cleaning. She would labor and her children would no longer go hungry. Perchance she would marry again and have more babes.

The clouds and moon left shadows on the ground, and the horse knew his way home. As they approached, Christian called out quietly to the guard. The gates were raised and he rode into the courtyard. The stable boy, rubbing his eyes, waited. Christian tossed him an apple he'd taken from the cellar. The boy accepted the treat with a grin; he would not speak of the night rides.

Yawning, Christian stopped in front of Ashley's door, listening. Assured she was sleeping, he went to his own chamber, weary from lack of sleep.

Yet slumber would not come, as he found himself looking at the moon, asking the fates to aid him. If he were free to woo Ashley, if she would stay, he would modernize the castle for her, give her all he possessed to make a home for her. Would it be enough, or would she stand at the window, looking into the night, longing for home?

Ashley woke, humming under her breath. She missed having music play through the room, like she missed a switch to fill the room with light. One of the servants had been in while she'd slept and stoked the fire, so the room was cozy. She was getting accustomed to being here—the cold didn't bother her as much as when she'd first arrived and thought she'd never be warm again.

The dress she had worn when she first arrived was packed away in the small trunk at the foot of the bed. Given it had a zipper and corset, she thought it best to hide it away, afraid it would attract too much attention, based on all the questions the girl had when she brought it back from mending and cleaning. Ashley had kept the story simple:

coming from a faraway land, clothes were made differently, though thanks to the damn dress, pockets were catching on. Not like the pockets they already had, slits in a dress or tunic allowing access to a purse or pouch attached to a belt, but real pockets sewn into the clothes.

"Sorry to whoever invented modern pockets." Then again, maybe these pockets inspired the person. Who knew? So the dress was packed away for safekeeping. She cast a glance at the dresses hanging on pegs on the wall. Not like she could manage by herself.

The girl, Gwen, would show up soon and help her dress. The water from the pipe in the wall was bracing as Ashley splashed her face and took a quick morning shower, as she called it, when really it was more like using a square of linen to wash, like a sponge bath.

How she missed hot showers, the steam filling the room on a cold morning, the heat of the water soaking into her skin. But the cold, it certainly got her going, and on the plus side, she no longer needed a cup of coffee to wake up in the morning.

There was a knock at the door, and Gwen entered. "Shall I dress you?"

"Please."

Christian had sent a merchant. Ashley couldn't believe all the choices and questions as to what she wanted. Apparently, she was to buy as much as she wished, but knowing she was going home, she only picked out material for three.

That same day, Christian had taken her to a small garden behind the chapel and showed her the sundial. It was interesting, but she no longer cared about the time. She'd come a long way in a month or so.

She'd missed not only Halloween, but Thanksgiving too! Then again, they wouldn't be celebrating an American holiday here. If she was stuck here, she was going to find a way to have her favorite holiday meal. There had to be ships bringing cargo—surely she could ask Christian to buy a few and allow a small path of garden, maybe near the sundial, where the potatoes could be planted? The thought of mashed potatoes with butter made her stomach growl.

"Mistress?" The girl held up the gray wool. "This one will look lovely with your hair and eyes."

The dress was made of wool and embroidered around the hem sleeves and neckline with leaves in silver thread. The shift and new cloak were also embroidered. The girl efficiently dressed Ashley, settling an ornate belt around her waist with a pouch dangling from it. Though hers was empty. When Ashley asked what it was for, the girl said the mistress of the keep would normally have keys and coins and other things that she kept on her person.

Ashley had one tiny rock she kept in the pouch. She'd found it walking one day. It was flat and smooth, reminding her of the marble counters in her apartment. She'd picked it up and kept it with her ever since as a reminder, not only of home and what she had left behind, but how she had changed. As the time passed, she accepted her new reality, decided to make the best life she could, whether she remained at Winterforth or went elsewhere.

As she sat on a stool while Gwen did her hair, Ashley touched the beautiful tortoiseshell combs Christian had purchased when the merchants had come calling. Gwen put her hair up using the combs. Ashley wished for moisturizer and body lotion. So far she hadn't seen any, but knew there must be a way to make the cream. It was something she would have to figure out; no way was she spending the rest of her life in medieval England without moisturizer.

She touched a hand to her hair. "Thank you, Gwen. It's beautiful."

"Lord Winterforth is in the lists. Are you going to watch him?"

"I wouldn't miss it. All that male prowess on display. Are you coming?"

The girl blushed. Ashley knew for a fact Gwen had quite the crush on one of Christian's guards. She thought the man's name was Ulrich, which in her opinion was a horrible name, but it wasn't uncommon for the time.

The girl chattered away as Ashley followed Gwen down the stairs, with Quinn waiting in the hall. Before they stepped outside, Ashley pulled the blue cloak tight around her and put the hood up, grateful the thick wool was lined with fur and kept her plenty warm.

Before. It was how she'd started thinking of her old life. As soon as it turned cold, people stayed inside, darting from cab to restaurant. Then they'd emerge in the spring, pale and blinking at the sun. Here, people were outside all the time, even when it snowed or rained. Then again, even with the fires blazing, it was chilly in the castle. Ashley blamed the abundance of fresh air, no more exhaust fumes, for the change in her mood.

The ring of steel and insults hurled about told her the men were already in the lists. She'd made an effort to pick up a bit of Norman French, and of course the insults and swear words were the ones she'd learned first. If she ever did make it home, she couldn't wait to use the best ones on her old boss Harry and, of course, Mitch.

"Over here, mistress." Gwen spread a blanket out over a stone bench. It was tucked into the corner of two walls so they were protected from the wind. They turned their attention to the spectacle in front of them.

Ashley had never considered herself one of those women that ogled the guys at the gym like her friend Marsha, but this… These guys were worth ogling. There were a few men shooting arrows at targets. Her eyes traveled over to the other men fighting hand to hand with daggers, and still no sign of Christian. Then she heard his voice.

"By twos, I wish to work up an appetite this morn."

Half of the garrison groaned as Christian strode into the lists, followed by Ulrich and Walter, and Ashley elbowed Gwen.

"Look, Ulrich is coming up next."

Gwen leaned forward, hands under her chin as she watched the man, her feelings evident on her face.

Watching Christian fight with his sword was like going to the ballet. It was a dance of beauty and grace. The blade seemed part of his arm as he fought Ulrich and another man. Ashley didn't know where he found such a reservoir of strength. He told her he'd held a sword as soon as he could walk, and she could believe it. Christian threw back his head and laughed as he sent one of the men's swords flying. Ashley pulled her legs up under her dress, wrapping her arms around her knees, content to watch. Even if he was engaged.

As she was thinking about what it would be like to live here with him, she heard the sound of horses. A carriage came to a stop in the courtyard.

Gwen pulled her up to stand on the bench. They had a perfect view as the carriage door opened.

Chapter Nineteen

As much as Ashley wanted to pretend it didn't matter, she craned her neck to see as the carriage door opened. The horses were all black, and the carriage had curtains covering the windows. It looked like it would probably be a bumpy ride, but it certainly would've been better than being on horseback for weeks on end.

Why couldn't Christian have been traveling in a carriage when she met him? It would've made their journey from Wales so much easier, and maybe they wouldn't have been robbed. Come to think of it, he always had guards around him, but he was traveling alone. As a merchant she didn't question it, but as a rich noble? Why?

An older woman stepped out first, dressed simply, probably the chaperone. The two men who had been driving the horses unpacked the luggage, and Ashley wanted to laugh. It looked like the girl packed more than Marsha packed, and that was saying something. Marsha would show up for a weekend trip with six or eight bags, while Ashley had one bag and one tote.

There had been a lot of speculation around the castle—she'd heard the girl wasn't a noble, but came from a family that Ashley would have called solid middle to upper-middle class. The father was a merchant who had made a deathbed promise to his wife to make a good match for their daughter.

The lack of sound had her turning to see everyone avidly watching to see what the girl looked like. Christian's steward, whom Ashley called the weasel, scurried forward to greet the women. Which guard would he assign to his future wife? Quinn cleared his throat.

"What?"

He grinned. "She's not as comely as you, lady."

Ashley rolled her eyes. "It doesn't matter, does it?"

His face turned serious. "Nay, I suppose it does not. 'Tis a shame. I rather thought Lord Winterforth would plight his troth to you."

"Go play with your sword or something," she grumbled at him.

Because really, her guard was just being loyal. The girl was breathtaking, with pale skin, an oval face, and a high forehead. Her hair was so blond it was almost white, making her gray-blue eyes look almost silver. She looked like a painting in a museum. For the first time in her life, Ashley felt like the frumpy middle-aged housewife who had let herself go and was now confronted with the mean girl from high school at their reunion who, of course, still looked perfect.

Christian bowed, and the girl nodded, but Ashley couldn't hear what they were saying from here. No matter; she'd seen enough. It was either go home or find a job here—well, not here as in Winterforth, but here as in the past.

There was only one place to go, a place in a million years she'd never dreamed she'd long for. The stables. The atmosphere there was meditative. Brushing the horses, talking to them. They listened and didn't talk back. The whole place calmed her. What did it say that she no longer thought the horses stank, and had come to like the smell of the stable and the horses? Talk about a change.

One of the boys greeted her, handing her a brush without a word. They'd come to know her routine over the past week or so.

The boys went about their chores, and during her days here, she'd noticed they tended to find time to sneak away and do heaven knew what. Not that she cared; she was glad for the privacy. As she brushed the old horse who had brought her to Winterforth, the one she had secretly started to call hers, she talked to him.

"Guess what I brought you today?"

The horse twitched an ear.

"That's right, I snatched a carrot. But don't tell the others. They'll be jealous."

The horse munched the carrot, and Ashley heard a noise. It sounded like her stomach, but her stomach wasn't growling. She whirled around but didn't see anyone in the stables, so she chalked it up to coming from one of the horses. It was warm and cozy in here with the horses, insulated from *him* and the decisions she needed to make. As she brushed the horse, she kept looking at the other stalls. Something was different. Then, in the empty stall next to hers, she saw the hay move. She tiptoed over, brave with the knowledge Quinn was only a scream away, and kicked at the pile of hay. A boy popped out, making her shriek.

Quinn appeared, sword drawn.

"Sorry, he scared me."

Her guard scowled at the boy. "Do not scare our lady."

The boy gulped. Ashley could feel him trembling as she held on to his arm.

"Thank you, Quinn. You can go back to whatever you were doing."

"Guarding you, lady." He winked and sauntered out of the stables.

She waited a few minutes before she let go of the boy and knelt down to look at him.

"You scared me and you frightened the horses. What are you doing hiding in here?"

The boy was dressed in rags. His hose had holes in the knees, while his tunic was too tight and showed a strip of skin at his belly. He wiggled, revealing bruises along his side, making her sick to her stomach. One of the marks looked like a handprint.

"I didn't steal nothing." The boy spat. "Let me go."

"How old are you?"

His eyes downcast, he shuffled his feet. "Six."

"Now tell me, how did you come to be here?"

"My parents left me in the woods for the fairies. I'm cursed." Bravado gone, a tear streaked down his dirty face, leaving a clean track of skin in the dirt. Brown eyes met hers, and deep within, something shifted inside her.

The boy pulled his hose down a few inches so she could see his hip. There was a large birthmark that almost looked like a flower.

"Why are you showing me your birthmark?"

"The mark of the devil, lady. I am cursed. The priest said so."

She took a handkerchief from her sleeve, dipped it in the water from the horses' bucket, and scrubbed the boy's face until it was pink and clean.

"I want you to listen to me very carefully. You are not cursed. Your parents were wrong to do what they did."

He was watching her seriously, but skeptically as well.

"I want to show you something."

With a glance around to make sure they were unobserved, Ashley pulled her skirts up to her knee, rolled her stocking down, and turned around.

She pointed. "It's not a curse. It's how you were born. Many people have them." She dropped her skirts and turned to face the boy. "Do I look cursed to you?"

"Nay, lady." He looked thoughtful. "Ladies shouldn't show their legs."

Ashley grinned. "No, they shouldn't. But we'll keep it a secret between us, shall we?"

The boy nodded.

"What's your name?"

"Merrick."

"I'm Mistress Ashley. How did you find your way to Winterforth?"

His stomach growled again. "I walked for a fortnight."

He said it so matter-of-factly that something about his acceptance of his situation broke her heart.

"Come along; let's get you something to eat, and then you can come back and help me finish brushing the horse."

He followed her into the kitchens, keeping close. The cook glanced at her and frowned.

"Mrs. Smith, I found Merrick in the stables. Looks like he could use a meal and a bath."

The boy protested.

"The cost of your meal is a bath."

He slumped, but nodded.

Mrs. Smith clapped her hands together, nodding at Ashley over his head. She had seen the cook saving scraps for the poor, knew she had a soft spot for the lost ones, as she called them.

"We will take care of him, lady."

The boy grabbed hold of Ashley's skirts, brown eyes beseeching. "Don't leave me here, mistress."

Ashley knelt. "I'm going to find Lord Winterforth and tell him you're here." Seeing his terrified look, she clarified: "Don't worry—you are under my protection, and he will allow you to stay."

She brushed a curl back from his face. "Do what Mrs. Smith tells you and don't make a fuss when they give you a bath. You are rather smelly. I think the horses smell better than you."

He gave her a tiny smile. It was enough.

Ashley whispered, "I bet if you're good, Mrs. Smith will find something sweet for you to eat after dinner."

She met the gaze of the cook, who nodded, wiping her

eye.

"One of the girls will come and fetch me when you're nice and clean. Then I'll show you where you can sleep."

The boy didn't speak, he simply nodded and watched her go, the look on his face one of utter desolation. It took everything Ashley had not to run back and pull him close, hold him tight, tell him she would protect him always. Never let anything happen to him and that he would never be alone again.

She was furious his parents would leave him, even though she knew how strong superstitions in this time were, and when she looked at it from their point of view, she could almost understand. She would keep him safe and tell him how to hide his birthmark.

It was early afternoon, so Christian was probably in his solar with the rodent steward, going over the books. As she raised her hand to knock, she heard low voices. There was something about the tone that made her pull her hand back. Christian's guards were nowhere to be seen, but Ulrich was always close, so she likely only had minutes until he came back. Knowing she shouldn't eavesdrop if she didn't want to take a chance on hearing something she didn't like, she put her ear to the door anyway.

"You must send her away, my lord. She is a temptress. You are to be wed. 'Tis not right to have your mistress under the same roof as your wife."

His mistress? Was that what people thought of her? Feeling sick, Ashley left without telling Christian about Merrick. She'd overstayed her welcome, and there was no way she wanted people gossiping about Christian. He'd had enough awful things said about him. As for her? What did she care what they thought? She sniffed and turned away.

Chapter Twenty

Ashley wasn't used to having free time on her hands. As someone who had worked since she was sixteen, this life of leisure was disconcerting. Seemed she lacked any useful skills—her college degrees would be useful for wiping one's rear and that was about it.

Cooking? Disaster. In fact, poor Mrs. Smith had banished her from the kitchen, telling her never to return, except, of course, for a lovely chat. It was good the kitchen was made of stone, or Ashley might have burned the whole place to the ground. The good thing about her brief time in the kitchens? Homemade pastries. Mrs. Smith worked with her to perfect them. A bit of jam inside and a sprinkle of sugar on top. Ashley liked them because she could put one in her pocket to eat later, as she'd found she wasn't hungry first thing in the morning. And while they probably should've been more of a dessert than breakfast, there was a lot of jam in the larder, so she figured it wouldn't hurt to have them now and then.

Crafts. The next fail. As a child she'd never gotten into crafts. Both her parents were solid lower-middle class, and worked all the time.

Reading had always been her greatest love, and while Christian had a large library, many of the books were in languages she couldn't speak. She guessed she could spend her time learning French, Greek, Latin, and Italian. Oh, probably German too. So she read the books he had in English, but she yearned for a good thriller to pass the time.

The servants were horrified when she asked to help clean, especially when she spilled the bucket. A housekeeper was provided for her dorm at school, and she'd always had a cleaning lady in the city, so that was another no-go.

When she tried the stables, she was firmly shooed away. It was fine for a lady to talk to the animals and brush her favorite horse, but nothing more.

So she'd taken to walking, as Christian did. He told her walking helped him think, and she'd found out from one of the guards that he liked to go riding at night. Now that was something she needed to add to her list. To become an accomplished horsewoman. She no longer worried about falling off every time she climbed on a horse, but she still couldn't consider herself accomplished, especially when she saw the little kids riding, putting her to shame. Then again, she'd like to see any of them try and drive a car. Or navigate the subways.

Ashley remembered when she was in London a year ago. She'd been on the tube and there'd been some guy talking to people. She could tell many of the passengers were annoyed, and she didn't blame them. Morning tube time was like your own precious bubble of space, and you didn't want to talk to anyone. The guy had said he was trying to change the culture. She couldn't believe how arrogant he was to think such a thing. He had said he was from Oregon, and she wondered how he would like it if someone from another country came to Oregon and started telling him what to do to change his culture.

With that in mind, she'd tried to be considerate. It wasn't her place to change the culture or people, as much as some things bothered her, like Merrick being left in the woods to die. She had always believed in trying to gather all the facts before making decisions.

The whole women's rights thing was a big issue, but she knew it was going to take hundreds and hundreds of years before anything really changed, though she'd figured out, the way Christian talked, that he and his family seemed to be an anomaly. They treated their wives well, and it seemed the wives had a great deal of say. So maybe it was a generalization to say women didn't have rights. Maybe women had figured out what women had always known. How to work within the confines of their lives to achieve their end goals.

Cloak pulled tight, she walked past the garden behind the chapel, smiling at the sundial. A group of children were gathered in a circle, heads bent, talking in excited voices.

"What do you have there?"

One of the boys hid a piece of paper behind his back.

"I'm not going to take it. I just want to see what it is."

The children shook their heads, and it was Merrick that

spoke.

"Nay, lady. 'Tis about the man in the cloak."

"What man?"

The tallest boy grudgingly thrust the paper out at her. "That's him, but we can't read what it says."

"Will you tell us?" one of the girls asked.

Ashley had wondered what they were doing, had figured they were up to no good. Had no idea they were studying what must've been some kind of a medieval poster, and was even more shocked they couldn't read. Then again, a lot of people were illiterate. She thought Winterforth was different.

"Give it here."

It was hard at first to make out the words, but after reading through silently a few times, she had it. As she read to them, the kernel of an idea sprouted. According to this, there was an unknown man who aided the poor. From what she read, it rather sounded like it was Robin Hood. But they called him the man of the cloak, and no one seemed to know who he was. If someone was in need, he helped. Widows, children sent to apprentice and learn a trade, young girls making good marriages—the man was a saint. Something niggled at her, but she pushed it away, focusing on an idea as she looked at the children.

"Can any of you read?"

They all shook their heads, and Merrick spoke up. "Nay, lady, we cannot."

Perhaps this was what she was meant to do with her time here.

"Would you like to learn how to read?"

Some of the children gaped at her, others looked at her

with suspicion and disbelief, but a few smiled. One of the girls stepped forward with a shy smile and took her hand. "I would like very much to learn how to read."

Ashley knelt so she was at eye level with the girl. Growing up, Ashley hated it when an adult towered over her and spoke down to her like she was some little thing that didn't matter. So whenever she encountered a child, she spoke to them like an adult, and on their level, eye to eye.

"Then I shall teach you."

One of the guards, a scary-looking man she had seen take down several men during daily sparring sessions, took a few steps closer. When he spoke, his voice was quiet and calm, at odds with his size and looks.

"Mayhap you would teach me my letters, lady?"

Ashley kept her surprise to herself. For some reason, she had assumed most of the adults could read. Christian took good care of his people, so she'd assumed, but that was what she got for assuming.

"Of course. I'd be happy to."

She looked around and found a twig then pointed to the boy most likely to have a plethora of weapons secreted away on his person.

"Could you make a point at the end?"

He nodded, pulled a knife from his shoe, and set to work. When he handed it back to her, she touched the point.

"Thank you. I think I could use this to kill a wild beast if I had need."

The children laughed, and Ashley noticed another guard had come to join the scary-looking one.

She decided she would start with something that would

appeal to them all. Instead of starting with all of the ABCs, she thought she would start with a couple of words.

So she smoothed the dirt with her foot and drew the letters for *sword*.

With the stick, she pointed to the S.

"Let's start with one of your favorite things. A sword."

There was murmuring and nods all around.

"This is the S."

And she went on, drawing and pointing to each letter, then having each one repeat what she'd done. She didn't know how much time had passed until the two guards stood tall.

"My lord," the scary one said.

"Mistress Ashley. What are you doing?"

Of course, he looked amazing. He wore a soft gray tunic and hose, the tunic beautifully embroidered. When she'd asked him why he didn't dress more ornately, he said he did when he went to court, but at home he preferred a simple tunic and hose—easier to fight in.

"I'm teaching the children and a few of your guards to read."

He blinked at her. "Aye, 'tis a good thing." Then he looked at the children. "Listen to your mistress and do as she bids."

A chorus of "ayes" answered him. Christian looked to both his guards.

"You may learn as well, if it does not interfere with your duties."

"Thank you, my lord."

Ashley dusted her hands on her skirts. "I want you all to practice drawing these letters in the dirt. Get a stick, sharpen the end, and practice the letters for *sword*. Now, how do we spell it again?"

As one they spelled the word, pointing to the letters. Ashley felt like a proud mama, watching her child take its first steps.

Christian offered his arm, and she walked with him as he talked about his day.

"I thought everyone here could read?"

"Nay. Why do they need to know their letters?"

So nobility was educated, the masses were not. She opened her mouth but then shut it. Different times. So she would teach those who wished to learn and change her tiny corner of the world for the better.

He asked her about the reading, and she went on to explain to him how she had felt useless.

"You're so full of life. Don't you find it exhausting?"

"Me? I would've never described myself that way."

Christian tucked a lock of hair behind her ear. "You are full of passion and life. You bring the sun to Winterforth."

"It's very nice of you to say." Ashley stopped him in the chapel garden. "There's something I need to say."

He waited, a brow arched.

"The other day, I was looking for you, to tell you about Merrick."

"Aye. The boy is doing well."

"Before that. I came to the solar, and I...I know it's rude to eavesdrop, but...I heard your steward say people think I'm your mistress. And that I should go."

Christian rubbed his chin. "Aye, you should not listen at doors. My steward is an old man. You are here under my protection. There is nothing untoward between us. The people here care a great deal for you; many have said so. They do not see you as such—if anything…"

"What?"

"They see you as Lady Winterforth."

"Oh." So not going there. "What about me leaving?"

"Your home is here."

"But your fiancée is here. Though where is she? I haven't seen her except at supper." Which she'd been fixing herself a plate in the kitchen and eating in her room so she didn't have to look at them together. *Coward.*

"Helen and her chaperone are keeping to their chamber. The girl is tired from her journey."

"Oh. I see."

Christian stared into the distance. "You love to read?"

"I do. When I was a child, I brought home armfuls of books every week from our library. So when I saw them discussing the man in the cloak, and found out they couldn't read, I figured I would teach them."

"The man in the cloak?"

They had walked to the meadow, where the stable master was working with one of the new horses. Christian leaned against the fence.

"Yes. He apparently goes around doing good deeds."

Christian was acting weird. "Don't you approve of him?"

"I do, but others might not."

He touched her cheek. "You have been outside too long and are cold. We shall go in."

Inside, Christian led her down a passageway she hadn't been down before.

"Where we going?"

He opened a door to a room filled with odds and ends.

"I will have the men clean out this room. You could use it to show the children and others their letters. Would that please you?"

"Very much." Ashley touched the smooth walls that were a dingy white. She turned to look at him. "Could we paint two of the walls a dark color?"

"Aye, why?"

"I saw someone using chalk the other day. If we painted the walls a dark color, they could write on the walls with the chalk, and then we could clean it off every day. Outside we can use the dirt to draw in, but paper is expensive, I don't want to waste it."

Christian nodded. "It shall be done. You shall have as much chalk as you desire. But why two walls?"

"I'll write the letters and the words on one wall, and they can practice on the other wall. When we are done for the day, one of the children will wash the walls and fetch more chalk as needed. That child may have one of the jam pastries."

Christian grinned. "They will be lining up to do your bidding."

He was standing so close that she thought she could count his eyelashes. The air grew heavy, and it was that moment of anticipation, when she thought he was going to kiss her. But he was engaged, his fiancée somewhere in the castle, and there was no way she would be called a home wrecker. Ashley quickly stepped back.

"Thank you. I'm going to go find a few of the children to start carrying everything out of the room."

He looked hurt. "I will send servants to aid you." Christian stopped in the doorway. "If I could change things..."

"Don't."

She lingered in the room until she was sure he was gone. This wouldn't do. He'd been more charming than ever. She couldn't stand him being so nice, and she definitely wasn't letting him kiss her and break her already cracked heart.

Ashley looked through the stuff in the room, pulling out a few stools the children could sit on and a table that was missing one leg. She'd ask if it could be fixed so she could use it in the room.

"I've got it."

She was going to act like a brat. Do all the things that she had seen her friends do that made guys lose interest. She picked up a cloth-covered bundle, and old, tattered ribbons fell out. Ashley grinned. She would enlist the little girls from her class to help. It was going to be perfect.

Chapter Twenty-One

The next morning, Ashley practically jumped out of bed, washed, and was waiting for Gwen to help her dress. The girl blinked at her.

"You're up early."

"Am I? Lots to do. Can't waste the day."

Gwen looked at her as if she was losing it, but didn't say a word. Once Ashley was dressed, she basically inhaled a bowl of porridge—or as she still called it, oatmeal—then took her place in the hall.

Where were they? A giggle sounded, and Ashley saw them. The three cute little girls were squatting down in between two of the tables that had been pushed back against the walls.

Soon enough, the garrison soldiers stomped into the hall, dark expressions on their faces. Ashley put a finger to her lips and the girls stopped giggling.

Christian stomped into the hall, bellowing.

"What is the meaning of this?" He brandished his sword, which now sported a pale pink ribbon around the hilt.

The men held up their swords, all tied with pretty ribbons. Ashley knew that bundle of tattered ribbons would come in handy. Those girls would make excellent spies.

Christian saw her and narrowed his eyes. A squeal escaped from one of the girls, and soon all three of them were shrieking and giggling. That was it—she lost it, laughing so hard that she wiped tears from her eyes. The men glared at them and grumbled as they removed the ribbons. Quinn and the scary guard—she blanked on his name—touched the ribbons and left them on their swords.

The girls snatched up the ribbons then froze, like baby rabbits hoping the hawk would keep flying and ignore them.

"What is the meaning of this?" Christian flicked the ribbon as if it were a dead thing.

Ashley straightened her spine. "We thought all of you would like them, that it would be pretty."

She purposely tried to look sad, wiping the smile from her face.

"Don't you like them? The girls and I worked so hard to pick out the perfect ribbons for each of you."

A couple of the guards looked sheepish and held out their hands to put the ribbons back. And the scary-looking one—that's right, Bryce—touched the ribbon on his blade.

Christian scratched his head. "'Tis rather fetching. I shall leave it. Will that please the lot of you?"

"Yes, my lord." The little angels said together, giving him their most innocent smiles. The ones Ashley knew they used right before they did something awful to the little boys of the castle. She covered her mouth with her hand as Christian and the other guards stalked out of the hall.

"To the lists, before we all turn into women."

Okay, so that didn't go as she'd planned. Ashley tapped a finger against her lip, thinking. A servant passed by wearing a length of rope as a belt around his hose. Of course—why hadn't she thought of it before?

"Girls? Might you know where we could get rope?"

Quinn spoke up. "Rope, mistress?"

"Yes, I need it for my lessons."

He looked dubious, but nodded. "Follow me."

Ashley gathered the girls close, whispering, "Meet me in the classroom and I will tell you what we do next."

The little girls ran from the hall as Ashley followed her guard. Once he had the rope, she led him to the classroom.

"Perfect. Now I need it cut into four pieces about this long."

Quinn shrugged and cut the rope. The girls had slipped in, and inched closer to the table, watching, so full of curiosity that Ashley thought they would burst. When he left they gathered around, touching the rope.

"What is it for, mistress?"

"Are we going to tie someone up?"

Another said. "Nay, we will trip them."

She grinned, making a note to stay on the good side of these bloodthirsty kids.

"We're going to jump rope."

There were blank looks all around. Ashley took one of the lengths of rope.

"Back up."

She gave it a couple of twirls, and after a few false starts—she wasn't used to jumping rope wearing a long dress—she got the hang of it. Like riding a bike. She threw in a few twists and crosses as the little girls cheered. When she stopped she was panting, sweat dripping down her ribcage.

"Would you like to learn?"

"Aye," they all said.

"Then this is what we shall do."

The next morning, Ashley and the girls were the first ones up. They'd eaten and hurried out to the lists. She had them practice some more, and hoped they'd at least get a few turns before the men came out to practice. She knew jump ropes had been found in ancient Egypt, Australia, and China. She didn't think it had hit Europe until somewhere around the 1600s or so, but she wasn't really sure. In the overall history of the world, what was a few hundred years? It wasn't like she was going to start a jump rope craze.

She and the girls had tied the leftover ribbons around the ends of the rope so it wouldn't chafe their hands as they jumped.

"Remember, elbows close to your sides and make small circles when you turn the rope, like I showed you yesterday."

She demonstrated with her wrists.

The girls practiced making circles with their hands and the rope, but not jumping yet.

"Good. Now make sure you're looking straight ahead, and don't jump really high, just enough for the rope to go under your feet. It should hit the ground as it goes under. Ready?"

Ashley thought she saw white-blond hair at the window above, but when she looked again the face was gone. Refusing to think about the impending nuptials, she showed the girls how to add a cross.

By the time the men appeared in the lists to practice, they were all jumping and laughing. Some men gaping, others cursing, and one went running, obviously to get the lord of the castle. Ashley ignored them and kept jumping. She hoped he would show up soon, because she thought she was going to have a heart attack. Whew, was she out of shape.

"Bloody hell, what is the meaning of this foolishness?"

Ashley turned to him. "Chrissy-poo, I'm showing the girls how to jump rope. Want to join us?"

He blinked. "What is Chrissy-poo?"

She smiled sweetly at him. "You are. Christian is Chrissy-poo. Isn't it sweet?"

Several of the men coughed and laughed. The grins disappeared when Christian scowled at them.

"All of you will pay for laughing."

A few of the men paled. Christian whirled back around, a scowl on his face.

"Nay, 'tis not sweet. 'Tis dreadful. The men needs train. You will move."

"No." Ashley shook her head. "This is the most open

space. We will be done soon. It's very good exercise. Perhaps some of the men would like to try?"

Bryce stepped forward, the yellow ribbon already grubby on his sword. Christian let loose a string of curses. Ashley was glad she wasn't fluent in Norman French.

"Cover your ears," she said to the girls, their eyes huge.

The guard stepped back, hanging his head.

"Nay, none of the men will do this jump rope. Begone," Christian thundered.

"You shouldn't swear so much in front of the girls." She coiled the rope around her arm. "Girls, come along. We'll find another place to practice. Let mean ole Chrissy-poo steal our fun."

As she turned away, Ashley bit her cheek to keep from laughing. She thought her plan was working. He looked incredibly annoyed with her.

"Mistress, you shouldn't vex him so. 'Tis not wise."

Ashley turned her most sugary smile on Quinn. "I'm going to make him wish he never laid eyes on me. By the time I'm done, he'll wish he'd never fished me out of that river."

"Ah."

"Ah?" She arched a brow. "Ah what, Quinn?"

The girls followed behind her, whispering to each other as they left the castle gates, crossed the bridge, and found a spot that wasn't too muddy.

Her guard looked wiser than his fifteen years. "You care for him, and as he is to wed another, you want him to despise you and send you away." He looked at his feet. "It will not be as you wish."

"How do you know?"

"I too wished someone to no longer care for me. It did not go as I wanted."

He looked so dejected that Ashley felt like the queen of the mean girls. She touched his cloak. "I'm sorry, Quinn."

"He cares for you. We all know 'tis so."

"I don't want to talk about it anymore. Want to jump with us?"

As Ashley showed Quinn how to jump, she thought about how she'd acted. Maybe one of his brothers would hire her to teach people to read? They'd be coming for the wedding and supposedly to tell her how she might go home. She'd find out about both. Then she'd decide. Should she stay or should she go?

Chapter Twenty-Two

Ashley had gotten used to waking up early. As long as it wasn't storming, she went out for a morning walk, finding she wasn't as bothered by the weather. It was still cold, but she welcomed the fresh air and the open space.

It had snowed again last night. With all the greenery decorating the hall, it looked like a fairytale castle. Christmas in a real castle. It would be magical. How was it possible she'd been here almost two and a half months?

The men would be out training today as well. They dressed warmer and went about their business, though everyone drank more warm wine. Her perfectly climate-controlled world seemed far away.

It wasn't like she could live off Christian's hospitality forever. Especially once he was married. As she was trying to figure out what she might be able to do to make a living, someone interrupted her.

"Mistress Ashley?"

She brushed the snow off the sundial and turned to see the last person she'd ever expected. Christian's fiancée.

"Hello."

The girl was even paler, almost the color of the snow. Had she been ill?

"I am Helen. Might we have speech?" The girl looked miserable.

"Of course. Let's go inside. I think we missed dinner, but Mrs. Smith will have saved us something."

Helen followed but didn't speak. Okay, what did she want to talk about? Had she heard the steward calling Ashley the mistress? Ashley glanced back at Helen—nope, didn't look like she was hiding a dagger.

They stopped in the kitchens and Mrs. Smith said she'd send a tray.

"Have you seen my classroom?"

"What is a classroom?"

"Come on, I'll show you." Ashley opened the door to the room. Christian had had another table and a few benches made, and someone had cut greenery and tied it to the window with a red ribbon.

"Please, sit."

Helen looked around, taking everything in. A servant brought them food and wine.

Ashley poured. "Drink. It's warm."

"You are teaching the people to read and write?"

"Yes, I think everyone should know how to read and write. Don't you?"

Helen looked startled, like no one had ever asked her

opinion before.

"My father taught me, but I think that was because he always wanted a son instead of a daughter. But none of the other girls I know can read or write."

She ate her stew, taking tiny bites, while Ashley practically shoveled it in. She was starving after being outside and jumping rope.

"Was there something you wanted?"

Helen put down her spoon and burst into tears. "I do not want to marry him. You must help me."

Stunned, Ashley sat there for a moment trying to figure out what to say. As much as she didn't want the wedding to go forward, she now knew how important it was for a woman to make a good match in these times, and Christian was as good as they came. He wanted to marry Helen, and so Ashley would do what she could to help, no matter how it shredded her heart to ribbons.

"Why don't you want to marry him?"

Helen buried her face in her hands, sobbing. Ashley scooted the chair over closer and patted the girl's hand.

"It can't be that bad. Why don't I tell you why he's a good man?"

Helen looked up and wiped her eyes on her sleeve.

"Lord Winterforth will listen to what you say. He will take care of you and look out for you. He is kind, and he'll make you laugh." This was payback for every mean thing she'd said or done, but Ashley took a deep breath and went on. "He's very strong. Did you know, I fell into a river and would have drowned. He saved me, carried me, and wasn't even breathing heavily. I know many men who couldn't have done the same. And have you seen him with a blade? To watch him fight is like a dance."

Helen had quit crying and was watching Ashley, an inscrutable look on her face.

"He's smart, and he believes in family above all else." Ashley took the girl's hand. She was young—maybe sixteen?

"And, of course, he's a noble with a title. And from what I understand, he's very wealthy."

"I know all this, lady. But I do not wish to wed him."

While Ashley had been trying to convince Helen, she had also been thinking about why she cared for Christian. How when she had talked about her job, he had asked questions, telling her that he knew she was successful and could run a household or army if she so desired. She knew he was the kind of man who would never hold her back. He might not always agree, but he'd support her and the choices she made.

She had told him about modern weapons and destruction. Not only guns, but the terrible bombs that were to come. He had wondered how she could live in such a time, and she had said the same to him, agreeing the weaponry of her time was capable of great destruction, but his time was more up close and personal with the violence. Though she thought her world was changing with all the awful things that had been happening lately. There seemed to be a new shooting every week on the news, to the point that she no longer watched, but figured if something really big happened, she'd hear about it.

"Helen, is there someone else?"

It was the only reason Ashley could think of why the girl would not marry him.

Helen shook her head so fast that Ashley thought it would pop off. And she suspected there was a boy somewhere waiting for her.

"I have heard what is said about him. I want children."

Ashley frowned. "You shouldn't listen to gossip. I know it is not true. It was made up by someone who was jealous Christian would not wed her." She refilled their cups. "And unless you have already had sex with a man and know yourself he cannot give you a child, then you would not know until you were married anyway, would you? And for that matter, it could be you that might not be able to give him a child."

Helen looked horrified. "Do not say such things."

Helen twisted the cup around in her hands back and forth. "I have not been truthful with you, lady."

Ashley gently took the cup so Helen would quit scraping it across the table.

"I think, given what you were talking about, that you can call me Ashley. Now tell me what's really going on."

Helen burst into tears again. It was a few moments before she could speak coherently. And when she choked out her story, Ashley sat there, frozen.

"So you see, I cannot marry Lord Winterforth, for I love another."

"Does your father know?"

Helen shook her head, fresh tears falling. "Nay, and he cannot. He promised my mother as she died that he would make a good match for me. I do not know what he will do if I tell him the truth. Can you help me? My father is arriving today."

And now Ashley was the one stuck. For she had been in a similar situation once before. Had been out with friends when she spotted the boyfriend of one of her friends. He was cheating on her friend, and when Ashley told her, she was the one who got blamed. To this day the girl hadn't spoken to her again. She was afraid if she went to Christian and told him, he might react the same way. Because he was obviously extremely touchy about all the broken engagements, and she was afraid this one might put him over the edge.

Helen was still looking at her, hope shining in her eyes. Ashley had to say something.

"We'll figure something out. Just give me a little bit of time." She patted the girl's hand

She didn't have a clue what it would be.

Christian had been looking for his betrothed everywhere. She had not come down to supper, instead sending her chaperone to tell him she wasn't feeling well. When he went to see how she was feeling, her chamber was empty. At the window, he saw a figure, the torches turning the pale hair to silver.

She was going to the chapel. Mayhap she wanted to see the place they would begin their life together. Once he was outside, he hesitated at the chapel doors. Who was his betrothed speaking to?

Christian slipped inside the door into the dimly lit building. He didn't recognize the man as his betrothed embraced him. 'Twas clear she was in love.

He sneezed, and the two jumped apart, guilty looks on their faces.

"My lord, I must explain." The boy bowed before him, holding out his hands.

Helen put herself between Christian and the lad as if he would cut the boy down where he stood. Had he been in love with her, he would have. She clasped her hands together in front of her.

"I was telling him goodbye. That I must obey my father and honor my mother's wishes. Mistress Ashley says you are a good man and will not beat me."

She was weeping. He patted her on the back helpfully.

"You love him?"

"More than anything."

Christian looked to the boy. "And you?"

"Aye, my lord. She is my life."

"My father knows I am in love with Caleb," she said. "He wants to be a carpenter—he makes beautiful furniture. But my father would not hear it, as he promised my mother he would make a good match for me. I miss my mother every day, but she would have wished for me to be happy, as she and my father were." Her shoulders slumped, and her pale face had red spots all over it. "But I will send him away and marry you if you wish it."

Christian rolled his eyes, wishing Ashley were here. She would know what to say. Why had she told Helen to marry him? Did she not care for him? He had fallen in love with her. He knew it when she was sick on his boots.

Christian sighed and frowned at the boy. "What would you do to care for and protect Helen?"

"I was apprenticed to a carpenter, but his cousin came and he no longer had a place for me. I will labor the rest of my life to take care of Helen."

"He makes such pretty chairs and tables." Helen took Christian's arm, smiling at the boy she loved. "Please do not make me wed you. I would not be happy."

Christian had only spoken to her twice since she had arrived. He thought her meek and quiet, but this girl, she had a will of her own, and he admired her for it. She reminded him of a certain woman with golden hair that was doing her best to vex him. Christian would not let her. And now he could make her his.

He held out a hand to Caleb, who took it as if worried Christian would chop it off.

"You make beds, too?"

Caleb nodded. "Aye."

"And you love her, will take care of her? Protect her with your body?"

Caleb nodded again, looking at Helen with love. "I will, my lord."

Christian made a decision. "Then say the words and I shall stand as your witness."

Helen wept.

"Cease."

She sniffed, wiping her nose on her sleeve.

"Do you, Helen, come to be with Caleb of your own free will?"

"I do."

Christian turned to the boy.

"And you, Caleb, do you come to Helen of your own free will?"

"I do."

"Then let you be joined together. Be happy and care for one another for all of your days." He looked to Caleb. "Do you have a ring?"

The boy reached in a pouch at his waist and came out with a plain silver band.

"Place it on her hand and let this ring bind you together for all time."

Christian clapped his hands together, happy for them both. "Caleb, kiss your bride. I stand here as witness, and will tell your father the deed is done."

The door banged open, and Helen's father ran toward them, wringing his hands. "Tell me 'tis not so? You dare to bring him here?"

Christian turned to the girl's sire.

"They are married. I stood as witness." The man raised his arm to hit his daughter, and Christian stepped in between them.

"I will see the boy set up to apprentice as a carpenter. I will send him to Nicholas Spencer, a cousin on my mother's side. They will be well cared for with Nicholas."

He took the pouch from his waist and looked inside, fingering the coin. Christian dumped a portion of it in Caleb's hand.

"Caleb, for you and your new bride."

The rest he gave to the girl's father. "Be happy for them.

Go home or go with them."

The father looked to Helen. "How could you do this? I promised your mother."

She hugged her father, weeping endless tears. "But Father, she would have wished me to find love, as you did. I care not for a title. I only want to be with Caleb."

He patted her on the back. "Then let it be so. For I will not have discord between us."

"But you could come with us. Lord Winterforth said so."

The father looked to Christian, who nodded. "I will put it in the letter to Nicholas."

"I can never repay your kindness."

"Go and be happy. 'Tis all I ask." Christian strode from the chapel happier than he had been since his betrothed had arrived. Now he must find Ashley. For he had much wooing to make up for, and he must woo her before he wed her.

Chapter Twenty-Three

Ashley woke to the sound of the gates opening. She jumped out of bed, the stone cold on her feet as she looked out the window. A figure rode out—it must be Christian going on one of his nighttime rides. In the light of the torches she could make out he was dressed in all black. Even the horse was black. It hit her. He was the man in the hooded cloak, playing Robin Hood. It had to be.

Pulling the dress on, she swore. It was difficult, but she thought the dress wouldn't fall off. Quinn had gone to bed, and the guard replacing him had fallen asleep. Not making a sound, she stepped over him and ran down the stairs. At the stables, one of the boys was yawning.

"I'm going with Lord Winterforth."

"He rides alone, mistress."

"Not tonight he doesn't."

The boy yawned again but did as she asked. Ashley was a

little unsure. Usually Christian was with her when she went riding. She leaned over and stroked the horse's silky gray ears.

"We need to find Christian. We can do this together."

She rode out of the courtyard, and when she got to the gate, the guard stopped her.

"'Tis late, my lady."

"I find I need to ride tonight. Open the gates."

The guard hesitated, and Ashley smiled sweetly at him. "Lord Winterforth knows I'm coming."

The guard nodded, blushing in the light from the torch. Great, he probably thought they were going to some secret rendezvous. Let him think what he wanted—she was more concerned with finding out what Christian was up to.

She was grateful the moon cast enough light for her to see the way. Her eyes quickly adjusted as she followed the path. As she rode into the village, she saw his horse, so she stopped and waited, watching. He went to the door of the home, opened it, and put something inside.

She was adjusting her dress when he rode past her.

"It is you."

Christian almost fell off his horse. It pleased her to catch him off guard.

"What are you doing out here? You could have been set upon by thieves."

"I heard you ride out and I knew it was you. But why keep it a secret? You're doing great things. I heard about the widow. And the girl you helped make a good marriage."

"Come, I will tell you as we ride home."

On the way, he told her all he had done.

"Can you understand?"

"You want something of your own. Not as a Thornton or Lord Winterforth, but as Christian. I think it's wonderful."

"I would ask you to keep my secret. Will you?"

"I will," she said as she reached across the distance between them and touched his arm. "I understand what it is to have secrets."

"Aye, many women do."

Her plan to be mean to him disintegrated to dust. He was a good man. Would whoever came up with the whole Robin Hood idea get it from the things Christian had done?

They rode in silence until he cleared his throat.

"There is much I must tell you. I am no longer betrothed."

"What do you mean you're not betrothed? I just talked with Helen today."

He chuckled. "I came upon her in the chapel with her love. Instead of running him through, I'm going to apprentice him to a cousin. He'll be a carpenter. And I gave them gold to start their life together."

"Why did she seek you out?" She told him of her conversation with Helen.

"You wished her to wed me?"

Instead of answering, she said, "I meant every word I said about you. So what now?"

"I would think it quite obvious."

And with that comment, Ashley was quiet. Did he really mean they would be together? And if she agreed, it would mean she truly had accepted staying. Giving up her life in the city, her job, and her five-year plan. She looked at the man riding beside her. He was good, strong, everything she could've ever wished for. Had he been in her own time, she wouldn't have thought twice. And then she knew: this whole time, nothing had felt like work. While her relationship with Ben had been hard and she was always thinking about it and how difficult she found it, with Christian everything came easy. They belonged together.

He stopped before they crossed the bridge. Dismounted. There was a charge in the air as Christian stalked toward her. He lifted her off the horse and, so slowly it was agonizing, set her on the ground, but didn't let her go.

When he bent his head to hers, her breath caught. He touched a finger to her lips, tracing the outline, then pressed his lips to her temple, hair, cheek, and finally, when she couldn't stand it another second, he tasted her, nibbling as she groaned deep in her throat.

Every cell hummed, tuned to him, as energy crackled and flowed from her into him. Ashley wrapped her arms around him and kissed him back, tasting mint and wine. The smell of him enveloped her, holding her close, and she felt like she'd crested the first hill on a roller coaster and was hurtling down the track. He was steel and satin as she surrendered.

"Pardon, my lord?"

Ashley jumped back with a yelp as Christian snarled and drew his sword. The guard looked sheepish.

"We were returning from night patrol and did not wish to disturb you, my lord. But the men are tired."

Mortified, Ashley recognized several faces of the guard.

Christian chuckled and swung her up on the horse in front of him.

"See to my lady's horse."

Over the next few days, Christian was never far away. He took her for rides, made sure she had met all the villagers, and even tried to jump rope. Medieval wooing was pretty spectacular.

She had finished her lesson for the day, proud of her students. They knew their ABCs and were working on bigger words. Yesterday she'd seen *bloody hell* written in the dirt and laughed, wondering who was responsible. Christian thought it was one of the girls.

A commotion outside made her look out the window. One after another, six carriages pulled into the courtyard. Finally she would meet his brothers and James and William. Though she was most looking forward to meeting their wives, as Christian had been uncharacteristically quiet about them.

"Ashley. Come. Meet my family." Christian practically dragged her outside. She couldn't help it—her mouth fell open. It was like a fashion shoot. The men all looked like models, and the women...they were pretty...but something about them... There were children and tons of luggage. It was total chaos.

"This must be your betrothed." A man with blue eyes and a rakish smile embraced her.

"Dolt. This is Ashley Bennet."

A woman stormed over, followed by a man with black

hair and a terrible scar.

"Christian Thornton, you've gone and lost your sixth fiancée? Hell's bells, I'm not finding you a seventh."

The man, who must be her husband, put a hand on the woman's arm as he stared at Ashley. "My love, I believe Mistress Bennett may be the one."

"Whatever." The striking redhead smiled. "It's nice to meet you. Sorry, it's just all we've heard is how this one wants to be married and we worked so hard to find this girl. Did you off her or something?"

It all tumbled into place at once. Christian being evasive. The women in front of her and the way they talked. The people in front of her went wonky. No, she was not going to faint. Instead, she narrowed her eyes and punched Christian in the arm.

"How could you?"

Then she faced the women. "You're like me, all of you."

Everyone started talking at once.

"Ashley, wait." Christian ran after her. Why had he not told her the truth? *Dolt, you didn't want her to go. Now you have likely lost her.*

She stomped into the stables, startling the horses.

"I should have told you about them. In truth, I was going to..."

"When? After you were happily married to Helen?"

"Nay." He held out his hands. "I do not know. All I know is I did not want you to leave me."

"How many?"

He did not know what she meant.

"How many are from the damn future?"

"All of the women."

She gaped at him. "Six women are from the future and you kept it from me?"

He'd never heard such words—well, mayhap his brothers' wives had said some of the words. She let out a breath.

"It's over. We're finished."

"'Tis you I want to wed." How did he make her understand how much he loved her? Could not live without her?

She whirled around, her eyes full of fire. "Don't you see? It wasn't your choice."

"I could not find the words." He had made a grave mistake. "Now you have met them, you can have speech together, they will tell you what they know, and you can choose." He took her hands, a sick feeling in his stomach. "Would you stay? Give up your life in New York? I would have a modern carriage made for you, give you everything I have to make you happy."

Her hands were so cold.

"Do not leave me."

"Just go, Christian. I need time alone." Her eyes were leaking, so he decided to seek the counsel of his brothers.

In his chamber, Christian opened the pouch at his waist, pulling the ring out. He'd had his men out searching ever since they were set upon by the thieves. Now the remaining three men were dead and Christian had the ring back, the one belonging to Ashley's dam. He wanted to rush back to the stables and offer it to her, but she was so angry. He would wait and try again, beseech her to forgive him.

And if she left him?

Nay, he would not think on it. The loneliness he thought banished was back, blackening his soul.

Melinda had never been so happy to see Christian smiling instead of moping about.

Ashley was the one he wanted, not Helen. She was dying to find out what on earth had happened since he'd left a couple of months ago. She and James had a bet—she thought the girl would run off with a sailor, but James picked a baker.

The way Christian looked at Ashley, Melinda would bet a pound of country ham he was in love with her. Which was fantastic, because Melinda had a feeling Ashley was the perfect match for him. She saw the way they looked at each other before Ashley stormed off. It was obvious they both cared for each other, so why hadn't Christian proposed?

Melinda had found Ashley in her classroom, teaching kids and a few of the guards to read. After the lesson, they'd talked over a few cups of wine, and she'd laughed when

Ashley confessed she had been mean to him on purpose to annoy him and put some distance between them both. Then everything changed, and Helen was out of the picture. And they all showed up. Leave it to Christian to not have told Ashley about them. So Melinda told her about meeting James and how her sisters met their husbands. They talked late into the day, and Melinda left determined to see them together.

Ashley couldn't believe there were six other women just like her. She really liked Melinda, appreciated her sharing her story and that of her sisters. But how could Christian have kept such an important thing from her? It was unforgivable.

Being here somehow felt like she had gone backward. Not just in time, but in her goals and dreams. To stay here in the past was to fail. In the future she had a good life. A fabulous apartment, a couple of good friends, an amazing job… Strike that. No more job. But she had plenty of money saved, and she knew she could find another job and another place to live. A better place.

Plenty of firms would be happy to hire her. She would be free to do as she wished whenever she wanted. No bratty kids screaming for her attention or a husband expecting a hot meal after a hard day at the office. At night she could sit on the counter, bare feet in the sink, eating cereal for dinner.

And on the occasional weekend day when she didn't go into the office, she would sleep half the day away, take a long nap and then a bath. She was answerable to no one, and it was the way she liked it.

The kids here would be fine. Someone else would finish teaching them to read, Christian would make sure Merrick was taken care of, and she would forget him.

In time.

The decision made, Ashley thought she could find a place in the village. She had her hair combs to barter. No matter what, she wasn't staying at Winterforth one more second. The old gray horse was nervous as thunder boomed across the sky.

"Ashley, halt."

Lightning flashed and the horse reared. She slid off, hitting the ground, a sharp pain slicing through her leg.

The sky opened up, rain stinging her skin.

Christian lifted her in his arms. "I've got her. Take her horse." He carried her to his horse. "Silly fool, you could have been killed."

"I hate you for lying to me."

He grunted and lifted her up on the horse. "You're bleeding."

"When I fell, I must have cut myself."

He urged the horse to a gallop. It wasn't until they crossed the bridge into the courtyard that she spoke again. "I want to go home."

There was a horrible sound, and lightning hit something outside the walls. From the smell, it must have been a tree. The smell of ozone was heavy in the air, the wind pulling at her. A terrible sound filled the air. This was it: she was going home.

But when Ashley opened her eyes, she was still here. The storm had blown through, a soft rain falling in its place.

It hadn't worked. She was bleeding and there was a storm. That was what Melinda had told her was required.

"It didn't work."

"I am sorry you could not return home. Say you will forgive me. I am a dolt." Christian reached in the pouch at his waist.

"What's that?" She squinted, holding the ring up to the torchlight. Ashley gasped. "I don't understand. Where did you find it?"

"I know 'tis all you have left of your dam. I have had men out searching since we were set upon by thieves."

She wiped her eyes. "Thank you."

He dropped to his knees in the mud. "I love you, Ashley. Say you will marry me."

Her stomach dropped. Talk about a hypocrite. She shook her head and pulled him to his feet. "I'm sorry. I can't."

Chapter Twenty-Four

The proposal changed everything. Now she was the one with the unforgivable secret. Over the next few days they avoided each other. Christian spent time with his brothers, while Ashley spent the days with Melinda and the rest of the women. She knew she had to tell him, especially after their blow-up. He deserved to know why she could not marry him.

They had taken over the ladies' solar thanks to Ashley. Charlotte was so happy they were all together, and would be for Christmas, hopefully with a new sister-in-law. Ashley was chewing on something. It had to be big. As much as Charlotte wanted to pry, she was trying to wait, see if Ashley and Christian would make up. But if they didn't soon, well, they'd all get involved. Shotgun wedding, anyone?

"You know, I don't know what made me think of it, but do you remember that terrible row between Aunt Mildred and Aunt Pittypat?"

Lucy looked up from her crochet, her silver hair pulled into a bun. Looked like she was making Ashley a scarf.

"I remember. We'd been there, what, about a month or so? You were hiding up in the tree, listening to them argue on the porch. I could see you from my bedroom window."

Charlotte knew Lucy would remember.

"She said something about a mystery man who washed up on the beach...but do you remember what else she said?" After pausing for dramatic effect and making sure her sisters were itching for her to tell, Charlotte dropped the tidbit in their laps.

"Aunt Mildred said the man was dressed strangely."

Melinda hopped up. "No way. Do you think it's possible?"

"Wait, what are you talking about?" Anna, tired from dealing with her son, who wouldn't sleep through the night, tucked her brown hair behind her ear and sat down next to Lucy.

"Tell us the story."

"Yes, do." Elizabeth and Jennifer shut the door behind them and proceeded to set up their easels.

Charlotte looked to her sisters. Lucy nodded.

"Our parents died in a sailing accident when we were little. I was eight at the time. Aunt Pittypat was kind of a hippie, and she took us in. Her sister, our Aunt Mildred, was always cranky and going on about how tired she was."

"Aunt Pittypat died of a heart attack the same day Lucy went missing," Melinda said.

"I'm so sorry," Anna said, and the others offered condolences too.

"Before she passed, did she ever tell you the identity of the mystery man? An old boyfriend?" Elizabeth handed Jennifer a small jar, and the two of them faced the windows to paint the winter landscape. They'd been painting scenes at each of their homes, and planned to do a painting for each season.

"We don't know. She would never talk about him, always changed the subject when we asked about the men in her life." Lucy's fingers moved quickly as she talked, and Charlotte always wondered how she didn't lose her place.

Charlotte had been thinking a lot about her aunt. She guessed it was natural during the holidays. "You know, she never married again after we came to stay with her. I always thought it was because of us." She grinned at the others. "After all, she'd been married eight times—it wasn't like she was opposed to the idea. But maybe it was because of him?"

"Do you think he could have been from the past? I wonder who he was. Do you think she let him go because of us?" Melinda frowned.

Charlotte didn't know why—it seemed to fit, but maybe that was because there were seven of them sitting together, all women from the future, yet here they were in the past, all having somehow found each other.

"If she did fall in love and let him go back to the past without her, I can't imagine how heartbreaking it must've been," Anna said.

Elizabeth turned around, a smudge of green on her chin to match her eyes. "Who was the youngest? Your mom?"

Charlotte nodded. "Yes, Mom was the youngest. Aunt Pittypat was the middle sister, and Aunt Mildred was the oldest. She was very proper and never married. When we went to her house, we were always afraid to sit on the furniture."

The memories washed over her as she thought back to that time in their lives when everything was so unknown, and how comforting it was to have her aunt accept them into her home, to love them as her own.

"The people here would call her a witch," Lucy said. "She liked to dance outside by the light of the moon, believed in ghosts, and I remember her talking to my parents every day after their deaths." She put her project down, wiping her eye. "Remember on Friday nights how we got to stay up late and hang out with all of her friends?"

Charlotte laughed. "She had the most interesting friends. Poor Aunt Mildred couldn't handle them."

A servant brought wine and pastries for everyone, and Melinda served, pouring as the scent of spices filled the air. "Remember Aunt Mildred's favorite saying?"

"No use borrowing trouble," all three sisters said together.

Charlotte looked at Ashley. "I used to say that the Merriweather sisters had the worst taste in men. Even Aunt Pittypat always said men were fun but they were more trouble than they were worth. She was a hippie with flawless manners, dancing naked under the full moon and then serving snacks afterward on china that was over two hundred years old."

Melinda jiggled her foot as she watched Elizabeth and Jennifer sketching out the scene. "I wonder if she and Aunt Mildred fell out over this mystery man." She wiped her eye. "Remember Aunt Pittypat used to say, 'Better shut your mouth before you swallow a bug, sugar'?"

"I wish I could have met her," Jennifer said. Charlotte thought she had the most beautiful hair, so black it was almost blue.

Charlotte had to swallow a couple times before she spoke. "She was right, though—she always used to say if you're in doubt about a man and your feelings for him, ask him to talk about himself or explain something. It worked for her, eight times." She put a hand to her neck, touching where the necklace had been, missed holding the charms in her palm. The necklace had belonged to Aunt Pittypat. It was a heavy gold chain with four charms. There was an emerald, a diamond, a sapphire, and one gold charm in the shape of a unicorn.

"Your aunt sounds fascinating. I'm sorry your Aunt Mildred wasn't kinder to all of you." Ashley had moved over by the fire. "I never had an aunt. My parents didn't have any siblings."

"We loved Aunt Mildred, even though she was annoying. The woman was set in her ways. I think sometimes when people get older and they live alone it tends to happen—a least, that's my theory." Charlotte looked over at Anna. "You've been sniffing a lot. I think you're getting sick."

Anna's nose was as red as a Christmas ball.

"Aunt Pittypat had a tried-and-true, never-fail hot toddy recipe. A cup of hot tea with a splash of whiskey, a spoonful of honey, and squeeze of lemon." Charlotte felt Anna's forehead. "You feel warm. I'm going to have a cup brewed for you."

"You have tea? And lemons?" Ashley said. "How did you get them? I didn't think they were in England at this time."

Charlotte resisted the urge to laugh. Ashley looked so excited at the thought of tea and lemons that you would've thought someone had given her a brand-new sports car. "James knows a guy. A sailor. And through some convoluted means, we're able to get them, though it takes forever."

Elizabeth turned from the painting. "You have to keep quiet about it. We don't want to change history somehow, in case some of the things we're doing cause tea and lemons and other things to come into general use earlier than they are supposed to. It might have some kind of strange ripple effect."

Ashley made the motion of locking her lips and throwing away the key. "I'll keep your secret. It might not be coffee, but what I wouldn't give for a cup of tea with lemon and honey."

Charlotte opened the door and spoke to one of the guards. "One hot toddy for Anna and tea for the rest of us. Don't worry; the girl I brought with me will be discreet."

Anna sneezed. "I hope it works. This is the first cold I've had since I've been here."

"It works wonders. You'll want to drink it three or four times a day, for a couple of days, and you'll be back to yourself in no time." Charlotte handed her a handkerchief.

Lucy looked out the window at the tiny flakes falling. "It's been the coldest winter I can remember since I got here, and the most snow I've seen. It's no wonder everybody's getting a cold." She looked at Ashley. "You'll have to work with your household to make sure everyone washes their hands. That's one of the most effective ways to stop the spread of germs and illness. Just tell them it's a ritual. That seems to work better than trying to explain germs."

Charlotte stood next to Jennifer and Elizabeth. "I love the snow. You know I'm going to want a winter scene for Ravenskirk." She turned to Ashley. "Make sure you shamelessly flatter both of them. They're incredibly talented, and we all have paintings they've done. Soon you will too."

Ashley looked like she was about to cry, so Charlotte changed the subject. As she looked at her sisters, and the women who had become sisters through marriage, her heart overflowed with love. Ashley would be part of the family, she knew it.

"I just know Aunt Pittypat would've loved traveling back in time. She was always up for new adventures."

"Couldn't you see her on the battlements under the full moon? Wherever she is in the afterlife, I know she's having the time of her life." Melinda blew her nose.

"We're sorry for being depressing, but today would have been Aunt Pittypat's birthday and she's on our minds. We wanted to remember her." Lucy let the tears flow.

Anna hugged Lucy. "Tell us more about her."

As Lucy told more stories, Charlotte touched her neck again. Though her aunt had never been one for material possessions, for some reason the necklace was really important to her. She remembered when her aunt went to Italy, attending mass at Easter in St. Peter's Square. The Pope gave his blessing, and it was said the objects that were there were also blessed. Charlotte and both of her sisters had always believed the necklace brought good fortune until it was lost.

As they ate, they shared more stories about Aunt Pittypat. The ache unbearable, Charlotte knew she had waited long enough. "I'm going to feed the baby and then I'll be back."

"I can't believe I'm sitting here talking to other time travelers. It makes me feel like we're all in a movie. Everything that's happened has been so surreal. I know you've probably talked about it a million times, but would each of you tell me how you ended up here and how long it took all of you to feel like this was home?" Ashley crossed her fingers as they answered, hoping she'd hear something that might help her with Christian.

Melinda groaned. "Better get comfortable, sugar. We're going to be here the rest of the day."

"And night," Jennifer added. "Wait." She jumped up. "Don't start yet. I'm going to get my sketchpad and capture all of us together. It will take a while, but I'll do a watercolor for each of us. To always remember this time."

Elizabeth joined her. "I'll help."

Anna finished her story, and then it was the

Merriweather sisters' turn. Ashley liked their maiden name. It fit them. As they talked and laughed, her throat closed. So this was what it was like to have sisters.

The next night after dinner, they were back in the solar. A fire crackled cozily in the hearth, which, of course, was big enough for all of them to stand next to each other. There were tapestries on the walls and the floors were done in beautiful tiles. When she'd asked, she'd been told they had come from Italy. Christian wanted them after seeing them at the other castles. They would've cost a fortune in New York.

Thinking of him made her feel sick. Ashley had tried to tell Christian but only ended up making things worse as he stomped out to the lists. She was thinking of enlisting the women's help when Lucy gasped.

"I almost forgot, which is crazy, because this is way important. Since I've been here in the past, I've asked everyone. And no one, not a single soul, knew anything about a curse."

Anna looked up from the yarn she was sorting for Lucy. "Do you think you made it up to help your future self?"

"Wouldn't I remember if it had already happened?" Lucy looked at all of them as they debated how time travel and time worked.

Melinda held up her hands. "You guys are making my head hurt. We keep going in a circle."

Anna dropped the ball of yarn she'd been holding for Lucy. "That's it. Time isn't linear. It's layered, like circles stacked on top of each other. When we fall through time it becomes our new present, even if we are in the past. So we wouldn't remember, because it's happening now."

Charlotte looked thoughtful as she tapped a finger to her lip. "You know, it makes sense. And it's the best explanation I've heard so far."

"Then you have to make sure the curse is strong enough that it will be repeated as the years pass." Ashley couldn't imagine believing in a curse, but then again, she had traveled through time, so who knew what else might be real?

Jennifer looked up from the easel, a smudge of charcoal on her hand. "Tell us the curse."

They all got comfortable in the chairs, blankets on their laps as Lucy settled back in a chair next to the fire, tucking her feet under her dress. As she did, Ashley caught sight of brightly colored crocheted socks.

"Simon Grey was Lord Blackford, the castle was practically a ruin, and his family had owned it since the 1300s."

"Homicidal jerk," Melinda added.

Lucy grinned at her. "Well, that's true, but if he hadn't been such a whack job, I might not be here. Might not have met William." They sat there for a moment thinking about what might or might not have happened if they hadn't all fallen through time.

"The curse said when the last of the Grey line betrays the

last of the Brandon line by foul deeds for the second time, the curse shall be lifted, and the castle owned no more by the Grey family. William is William Brandon, Lord Blackford, and I thought Simon was crazy for thinking I was a Brandon."

"I've got chills," Anna said. "So what was the second time?"

Charlotte's girl brought tea, and when she left, Lucy continued.

"I think the second time was when Clement Grey, his ancestor, tried to kill me by drowning me in the cistern on top of Blackford. I was saved by a raven."

A look passed between the sisters, and Ashley made a note to ask about the raven later. She was afraid that if she asked now, they'd go off on another tangent and she'd never hear all the time-travel stories. What would be a five-minute story to a New Yorker was an hour or more to a Southerner.

"And we know it worked," Melinda said. "Because when I went to the castle, the people in the village said there hasn't been a Lord Blackford since the 1500s. And they were named Brandon, not Grey. The last Lord Blackford was named Winston Brandon, and he died in 1564. The castle went to the National Trust."

Her hand trembled as she lifted the cup. "Winston was our dad's name. Simon believed that if he killed me, he would be free of the financial drain of the castle and able to enjoy his money. Of course, at the time I didn't know I was a Brandon because I was a Merriweather."

"The jerk sent a hitman after Melinda and I," Charlotte said. "And when we came through, it was twenty years after

Lucy."

"It's true," Lucy said. "I came through in 1307. And from all of our stories, I'm the only one who came through earlier than the rest of you."

Anna wiped her eye. "It's because William was meant for you and was waiting. You came through when you needed to."

Ashley sipped the tea, letting it warm her from inside. "You were either brave or crazy to go through with the fake wedding."

"I know, right? But you know, he could be so charming, I swear that man could convince a tiger to go vegan. So I went along with it, thinking it was a way to end things on a good note. Who would've known the guy would drug the champagne? I still miss that sparkly blue shoe."

"Well, I think it's poetic justice that he came through time with you and was smashed to death on the rocks. Dead as a doornail," Melinda said.

"You have to make sure you start rumors about this curse. Have your children and their children tell their descendants, and make sure it happens on the Grey side too." Ashley took another sip of tea. "Because could you imagine if somehow the curse was forgotten and lost over time? Would Lucy suddenly disappear?"

"I don't think so," Elizabeth said. "I think this is her new reality, and somehow it's already done, so even if someone forgot it, she would find out another way or go back another way."

Ashley held up her cup. "I think we need to switch to wine."

Chapter Twenty-Five

Charlotte was careful not to slip on the icy patches as she made her way across the battlements. Looked like it was going to be a rough winter. Were the severe climate changes and storms continuing to worsen at home? The summers had been hotter, with terrible flooding and hurricanes, and she hoped it had gotten better, that people had woken up and made changes to leave a world for their children.

She was staring at the ice on the trees when she heard a sound she hadn't heard in a very long time. A raven was flying low and close. One of the guards crossed himself and prayed as the big black bird almost clipped the guy.

The raven flew so close that she could see the iridescent feathers, and as it passed, the bird dropped something. She reached out without thinking to catch it. It was some kind of chain. When she opened her hand, a sob escaped, her vision blurred from the tears streaming down her face. How was it possible? She thought she'd never see it again.

Aunt Pittypat's necklace. Charlotte shielded her eyes, the chain dangling as she yelled, "Thank you, Aunt Pittypat. I love you."

The guard moved away, crossing himself again, but she didn't care. She ran through the corridors to the solar, shouting for her sisters.

Lucy opened the door, a look of alarm on her face. "What's the matter? We heard you yelling."

Charlotte could hardly speak, she was crying so hard. The charms sparkled in the light as she held up the necklace. After she'd blown her nose and wiped the tears away, she was able to tell them.

"Remember the ravens?" She looked to Melinda and Lucy. "Now I know. It had to be something to do with Aunt Pittypat. I don't know if she's up above watching over us, or somehow she was reincarnated as a damn raven, but one thing I know for sure: this has to be her doing. I'm so sorry I lost it in the well." Charlotte was crying again, holding out the necklace to her sisters.

Melinda took it and dropped it in her hand. "The raven gave it to you. It's yours."

"Are you going to tell us the story?" Ashley said.

Charlotte held the necklace up. "I had it last, so let me start."

After that emotional display this morning, Ashley had decided she had to tell Christian the truth if there was any hope the two of them might have a future together, and if not, at least she'd tried. She found him in the lists.

"Would you walk with me?"

He kissed her hand under the watchful eye of his brothers.

"Shall we come along, Ashley? Make sure our brother is comporting himself as a knight should?" Robert called out.

She was about to answer when Christian scowled. "The lady wishes to have speech with me. We do not want you lot loitering about."

He said to her, "'Tis too cold for you to be out walking. Come inside, where it is warm."

She followed Christian to his solar. When he closed the door, she took a deep breath to gather her courage.

"I'm sorry for everything. I have something I need to confess."

The hopeful look left his face, and she knew he was probably afraid she was going to tell him she had a secret husband or was running off with a merchant, so she had to spit it out before he kicked her out.

"Where I came from, I was always focused on getting ahead in life. And I always believed you could be whatever you wanted to be. But I was lying to everyone. I told them that I grew up wealthy, when in fact I had a terrible childhood."

Christian took her hand. "Are you married to another?"

"Nay." She shook her head.

"The night you sang in the inn...you had much to drink and you told me of your mother. The man and woman who made you their own."

"I don't remember much of the night. Why didn't you say anything?"

"We all have wounds that are slow to heal. We will heal old wounds together."

She didn't know what to say. He'd known about her childhood all this time and didn't care. Cold bloomed in her chest. Had she told him the other thing?

"Wait." She paced in front of the fire, skirts swishing as she walked. "When I ended up here in medieval England, I felt like I had gone backwards. The thought of living in a place where people were content to stay in one town their whole lives—it felt like failure. All I could think about was going back. Now I know I'm not a failure, where I lived doesn't matter, and it's who I've become that matters." She held out her hand. He took it instantly.

"I found something different here, something that banished the darkness. I found you, and Merrick and your family, and realized that's all I need in life."

"Then make me complete. Marry me, Ashley Bennett."

A tear slipped down her face. She wiped it off, but another followed.

"I want to. But I cannot."

"Why? Do you not care for me?" His hands had turned cold, chilling her through. "Mayhap in time, you would come to care for me?" Christian wiped her tears away with the pads of his thumbs.

She cried out. "I care plenty. It isn't that at all."

"Then what is it, my love? Together there is nothing we cannot overcome."

"I can't have children," she whispered.

"I did not hear."

Ashley bit her lip. "I cannot have children."

Christian looked confused. "How can you know such a thing?"

She took a deep breath. "When I was fifteen, I was in a lot of pain. My mother took me to the doctor and I had to have an operation. Surgery. They cured me, but the result was I cannot have children. And the funny thing was, I never cared. Not until I met you."

Her throat was raw, and she swallowed, trying to find the words.

"I know how much you want children and a big family. So no matter how much I wish to marry you, I cannot. You have my blessing—find someone else who can give you the children that you long for."

As she looked into his eyes, she saw him as timeless as the castle around him. A bit worse for the wear around the edges, but standing. And she knew he would never leave her. He would always be there to catch her. That was why she had to send him away, so he could have a chance at happiness.

Christian was silent for so long that Ashley knew she had her answer. She disentangled herself from his arms and walked to the door, her heart shattering like the icicles on the trees.

"Stay." He caught her up in his arms. "I have been a fool. All this time, I thought if only I had a big family I would no longer feel lonely. But I do not need to fill Winterforth with children. All I need is to be loved and to love. Tell me you love me, for that is all that matters in this world."

Ashley was crying so hard that Christian's face was blurred by her tears. "Of course I love you, but what does it matter? You aren't thinking straight, and you will resent me as the years pass when you realize you want children and I cannot give them to you. You must let me go."

Deep in her core, Ashley knew it didn't matter where she lived or who she pretended to be. All that mattered was the kind of person she was. She was Ashley Bennett, and she accepted her past, embraced this better version of herself, the woman in love with a man who was more than six hundred years older than she. A man she loved so deeply that she was willing to sacrifice her heart for his happiness. Somehow, she'd found the strength to let him go.

"I will never let you go. You are the other half of my soul. And you may not believe I would change my mind, but I know in my heart I do not need children. I only need you. Now say you will marry me."

She looked into his eyes, saw the love for her reflected within, and felt peace flow through her.

"Yes, I'll marry you."

Christian swung her around. "I will love you for the rest of my days. Together we will be our own family."

He captured her mouth, bruising her lips, claiming her as his tongue traced her lips and met hers in a dance as old as time. Their souls joined, the light banishing the darkness. Ashley had come home.

Could her life get any better? Today she was getting married, and tomorrow was Christmas Eve. She stood in the chamber letting the girls dry her off after her bath. Never in a million years was this how she would've imagined her wedding. Of course, she'd never thought of her wedding at all, but it certainly wouldn't have taken place in medieval England in a castle.

Anna had given her herbs to put in her bath, and Elizabeth had given her some lotion. Ashley begged for the recipe, and Elizabeth laughed, saying it was one of Aunt Pittypat's—the sisters had figured out how to replicate it with what they had on hand, and would share it with her.

For the first time in her life she had sisters, or would soon have. Ashley choked back a sob at the thought. Women she barely knew felt like family, and they were all here to see her marry Christian.

There hadn't been time to have a new dress made. They wanted to marry while everyone was here. With a critical eye, she looked at her dresses. Any of them would do, so which one should she wear? The sound of the door opening made her almost drop her cup of wine. All six women came in, their hands full.

"You don't think we'd let you get ready without us, did you?" Charlotte said.

"We've all brought something." Lucy smiled.

Melinda added, "You know, something borrowed,

something blue."

Ashley willed herself not to cry. "I don't know what to say. You all have been so kind to me."

Anna held up a pair of shoes. "I think we're the same size, and these would look so pretty on you."

Elizabeth held up a dress. "When we were leaving, I packed this. Not for Christian's other bride. I didn't know why I did, but now I do. It should fit if you'd like to wear it. And I think we're the same size in dresses, so this should fit if you'd like to wear it."

The dress was exquisite, pale velvet, covered in pearls and other semiprecious stones.

"It's the most beautiful dress I've ever seen," Ashley said.

Jennifer held up a pair of earrings. "I bought these at the last market day. The emeralds will match your eyes."

Lucy handed Ashley a bundle wrapped in fabric. "Go on, open it. I finished it late last night."

Ashley sat on the bed and opened the bundle. Inside was the most beautifully crocheted cape. It was a soft gray wool, thick and heavy. It looked like something she would have paid thousands for back in New York. She pulled it over her head and hugged it tight. She'd never been a crier, but the past few days? Nonstop tears. Of sadness and joy.

"Thank you, Lucy. I think it's the most beautiful thing I've ever owned."

Charlotte handed her an embroidered handkerchief. "Don't cry. Your face will get all red, and Christian will wonder what we've been doing to you."

Ashley dipped it in the cold water and blotted her face and eyes.

"I've come to realize that home isn't a place. Home is made up of the ones you love. They are your home no matter where or when you are." She blew her nose. "It isn't just Christian. I know it's only been a short while, but I consider all of you family. You have made me feel like I belong. I can never thank you enough."

"Now you're making all of us cry," Anna said as everyone wiped their eyes.

Charlotte took something out of her pocket and held up a necklace. "I want you to have this."

Ashley shook her head. "Charlotte, I can't. That's Aunt Pittypat's necklace. The one you guys were talking about."

"Then borrow it for the ceremony. I know she would be so happy you're wearing it."

Ashley nodded and let Charlotte put it over her head.

The women formed a circle around her. The comments came one after another.

"You look beautiful."

"The perfect bride."

"We're so happy you're here and part of the family."

Ashley thought this had to be the most perfect day ever. She took a deep breath. "I think I'm ready."

"Great. Let's get you married and celebrate." Melinda laughed. The door opened, and they preceded her down the hall. She was actually getting married. Ashley Bennett, the girl who thought she would never marry, had finally found a man she not only adored as a friend, but loved with all her heart.

Chapter Twenty-Six

The doors to the chapel opened. She heard the sound of a harp, and smelled juniper and beeswax from the candles. The scent of cinnamon and cloves filled the air. The chapel looked like something out of a fairytale, covered with greenery and candles. The wedding was to be family only. Afterward, they would join the rest of the castle in the hall for a feast with music and dancing.

Her soon-to-be sisters were dressed in beautiful gowns of every color, their jewels sparkling in the candlelight. And the men... Though all were handsome, she only had eyes for one.

Everyone was watching her. Ashley stumbled and straightened her shoulders. Somehow she made it to the front of the chapel where the priest waited. Christian mouthed, *I love you.*

"Tonight we come together, celebrating two souls joining together. Without love, life is meaningless; without love, death has no redemption."

The priest nodded to Christian as a rumble of thunder sounded outside.

"Join hands. Above you are the stars, below you the earth. As time passes, let your love be as constant as the stars, as firm as the earth. Be close to one another, have patience and understanding, for the storm will come. Together you will bend, not break."

She was so full of emotion she felt the earth rumble.

"What was that?"

Ashley thought it was Charlotte who spoke. So it wasn't just her. Everyone was looking around and at each other. And Ashley noticed each of the women were pale and watching her very closely. But she'd already survived a storm, and nothing had happened. It was fine.

The priest cleared his throat. "Place the ring on her finger."

She felt something cool slip over her finger, a momentary pain and warmth. She looked down to see a gold ring with an emerald. It had hit a scab on her knuckle, as she watched, a drop of blood welled up.

Then the priest handed Christian a cup. "Drink and bind yourselves to one another."

The wind screamed. There were nervous looks, but no one said a word. Christian drank and handed her the cup. She looked at her hands, the ring from her mother on her right hand and the gold band with the emerald from Christian on her left. She'd felt awful she didn't have a ring for him, but he told her not to worry; she could surprise him later. Ashley drank from the cup and handed it back to the priest, yet it was if she were in two places, here and back in New York. She could see it all so clearly, hear the sounds of cars honking and people shouting, the subway as it rumbled down the tracks, taste the food from her favorite restaurants, and see her apartment with its big windows.

The priest adjusted his robe and looked to Christian, nodding. "I now pronounce you husband and wife. May your love endure any storm and serve as a guiding light in the darkness."

The rumbling came again, and she heard thunder. It was like she was half awake and half dreaming as she saw her new family surrounding her, the man she loved in front of her, and yet she *could* see her home. The streets filled with traffic, the smell of the exhaust, overlaid with the smell of the greenery and beeswax here in the chapel, made her nauseated. She heard a scream, but wasn't sure if it came from her or someone else. She felt like she was floating, and Ashley looked down to see that she seemed to be shimmering. Was she dreaming?

She reached out for Christian, and from far away heard him call, "Come back. Don't leave me."

She tried to focus on him, but the sounds were so loud. She turned her head to look.

Someone called out, "Ashley. Focus on Christian."

But she wanted one last look.

Christian had been pleased with himself for getting Ashley to agree to marry him. They were almost to the end of the ceremony, and he had finally convinced himself she would not run at the last moment, when something odd happened. He had taken the ring and slipped it over her finger. But when he did so, it hit where she had scraped it against the stone wall yesterday, and he watched as a drop of blood welled up and fell to the floor. It was then that the earth rumbled, and as he took hold of her hand, trying to comfort her, he watched his hand vanish.

He would not let go of Ashley even as he felt a great pull. His arm vanished, and Christian heard terrible sounds. He saw everyone in the chapel, but also saw something else.

Strange horseless carriages he knew must be cars. It was as if he had one foot here at Winterforth and the other with Ashley in her world. He looked down to see he was still holding her hand. Yet when he looked up at her, she was still, like the stone walls of the castle.

"Ashley? Do you wish to stay?"

She looked at him, tears streaming down her face. "What do you want?"

"I want to be with you. I care not where. If you wish to go home, I would follow. I would follow you anywhere. Without you, I have no home."

She turned her head, listening. "They're calling for us. I've never had sisters or a big family." She took a deep breath and one last look, as if she were committing every sight, sound, and smell to memory. The sound of the great horseless carriages and the smells made Christian clench his jaw.

She took his other hand in hers and looked up at him, love in her eyes. "You are my home. Shall we?"

Christian came to sitting on the floor of the chapel, Ashley in his arms. He looked up to see everyone standing around them and the priest on the ground beside him.

"He fainted," Edward said.

"We'll tell him he had too much to drink before the ceremony," James said as William and Robert helped the priest to his feet.

Christian pressed his lips to Ashley's. "Wake, my wife."

She blinked a few times and focused on his face, smiling. Christian felt his heart open wide. They had each other, the love of their family. Nothing else mattered. They were complete, and Christian would spend every day of the rest of his life telling her how much he loved her.

"Thank goodness we only have family at the wedding," Lucy said.

Melinda added, "Can you imagine trying to explain what happened?"

William clapped Christian on the back. "Watching you vanish, I was more scared than when I fought my first battle. We could hear the sounds but could not see what made them. All I could think was that this is what Lucy had come through to be with me. You are a brave man."

Christian was overcome. He wiped his eye. "Dust. I have dust in my eye."

"You can put me down now," his wife said.

"Nay, I wish to keep you close."

"Well, as long as you put me down when we get inside. I'm starving."

Christian laughed, carrying his wife out of the chapel and into the hall, where they would begin their new life together.

Ashley laughed as Christian kicked open the door to the bedchamber. Candles flickered around the room like some kind of fairytale. There was juniper tied with ribbon and wine waiting for them. Her sisters had outdone themselves.

"My Lady Winterforth."

He laid her down on the bed, staring down at her, and while Ashley had boyfriends in the past, being in love made everything feel like it was the first time.

"Not only are you beautiful outside but you have a beautiful heart, my love." He removed her shoes, smiling when he saw the embroidery on the tops of her stockings.

"Melinda thought it was funny to embroider little swords and hearts on them."

He kicked off his boots and climbed up on the bed, stretching out next to her.

"If you ever left me, I could not breathe. When you started to go, you took the air with you. You are the air to me, Ashley. Don't ever do that again."

"I saw you there with me. And I knew we belonged here, with our family. I will never leave you. We'll grow old together."

He tucked a lock of hair behind her ear. "I will keep you safe, treasure you, and love you."

She wiped her eyes. "Don't make me cry. It makes my face all red."

"As you wish."

And they spent the night loving each other, knowing they had the rest of their lives together to learn what made them both sigh with pleasure. As the night deepened and turned to dawn, Ashley curled up next to her husband and fell asleep, perfectly content.

Chapter Twenty-Seven

Two Years Later

Ashley couldn't believe two years had passed. Lucy's son had another child, her eighth grandchild. It was only a few weeks until Christmas, and they had traveled to Somerforth to celebrate the birth of Jennifer's first baby. She had a boy, and Edward had been strutting around before dragging his brothers, William, and James out in the cold to cross swords in the lists. Which was better than them wrestling in the hall. The last time they'd broken a chair and Jennifer had shouted at them.

She and Christian had taken Merrick in as their own. He was now eight years old, and with his brother and sister they made a nice, happy family. The year after they took in Merrick, they'd met a girl at a market where her father was beating her. He'd offered to sell her for a paltry sum, and

Ashley had been horrified. Christian paid the man and they took the girl, Mary. It was only a few months after that they came across Arthur, he had been in a shipwreck with no survivors. While Ashley had never thought she wanted children, she had never been more fulfilled.

As much as she loved her life when she was single, she finally understood what her friends had been trying to tell her back in New York. She had always thought she wasn't meant to have children. Some people were meant to be single. While she still believed that was true, she also knew the love she had for Christian had profoundly changed every cell, her DNA. Maybe it took the right person to change. Seeing how happy Christian was playing with his sons and his daughter, showing them how to swing a sword, to go riding and hunting, made her smile every day.

At first she had been appalled he wanted to teach his daughter to use a sword, but she'd quickly given in when she saw how much Mary enjoyed spending time outside with her brothers and her father. The children, when they weren't following Christian around, trailed after the guards, asking a million questions. Ashley was happy they had not gotten into as much mischief as her sisters' children.

She remembered the stories of how they had taken Elizabeth and Jennifer's paints and painted the dogs.

Though Mary had come in last week with a basket full of kittens. She'd traded a basket of eggs for them. Ashley simply laughed and told her she was responsible for taking care of them. She guessed that at least when the black plague came, they'd have plenty of cats to keep the vermin away.

She and her new sisters had talked a great deal about

what was to come and what they could do to prepare.

They had also talked more about Connor. They speculated on where he might have ended up. So much had changed. Her life before had been empty, and she'd floated through life existing but not living.

Christian had teased her the other day about the time. Ashley couldn't fathom how she had been so obsessed with what time it was. What did it matter? The day dawned; life went on. She was so grateful to whatever power had brought her to the past and given her a chance at love.

Her husband had hired men from Italy to build them a conservatory, where she was growing tea and citrus. The men had done the same for his brothers. They had all decided they would not sell any, and only use what they grew for household purposes. Together they had decided it was the least risky way to impact history.

She was in the conservatory, looking at the plants, when Lucy came in. Ashley wondered how it must be for Lucy to see her sisters, knowing they were twenty years younger than she. Though Lucy said she still woke feeling as if she were in her twenties.

Ashley wished she could capture time, put it in the box and lock it away. To keep it from moving forward. For she wanted this time to go on forever. To savor every moment of every day. But even she had learned it was impossible to hold time in her hand. So she would live each day as though she might not wake to have another. Never again would she take anything for granted. Ashley had a home, she had family, and she had a love that would last until her dying breath and beyond. There was nothing else she needed.

Books by Cynthia Luhrs

Listed in the correct reading order

THRILLERS
There Was A Little Girl
When She Was Good - January 10th, 2017

TIME TRAVEL SERIES
A Knight to Remember
Knight Moves
Lonely is the Knight
Merriweather Sisters Medieval Time Travel Romance
Boxed Set Books 1-3
Darkest Knight
Forever Knight
First Knight
Thornton Brothers Medieval Time Travel Romance
Boxed Set Books 1-3
Last Knight

COMING 2017 - 2018
Beyond Time
Falling Through Time
Lost in Time

My One and Only Knight
A Moonlit Knight
A Knight in Tarnished Armor

THE SHADOW WALKER GHOST SERIES
Lost in Shadow
Desired by Shadow
Iced in Shadow
Reborn in Shadow
Born in Shadow
Embraced by Shadow
The Shadow Walkers Books 1-3
The Shadow Walkers Books 4-6
Entire Shadow Walkers Boxed Set Books 1-6

A JIG THE PIG ADVENTURE
(Children's Picture Books)
Beware the Woods
I am NOT a Chicken!

August 2016 – December 2017 My Favorite Things
Journal & Coloring Book for Book Lovers

Want More?

Thank you for reading my book. Reviews help other readers find books. I welcome all reviews, whether positive or negative and love to hear from my readers. To find out when there's a new book release, please visit my website http://cluhrs.com/ and sign up for my newsletter. Please like my page on Facebook. http://www.facebook.com/cynthialuhrsauthor
Without you dear readers, none of this would be possible.

P.S. Prefer another form of social media? You'll find links to all my social media sites on my website.

Thank you!

About the Author

Cynthia Luhrs writes time travel because she hasn't found a way (yet) to transport herself to medieval England where she's certain a knight in slightly tarnished armor is waiting for her arrival. She traveled a great deal and now resides in the colonies with three tiger cats who like to disrupt her writing by sitting on the keyboard. She is overly fond of shoes, sloths, and tea.

Also by Cynthia: There Was a Little Girl and the Shadow Walker Ghost Series.

Made in the USA
San Bernardino, CA
31 July 2017